About the Author

Malcolm Blair-Robinson is the grandson of an East Prussian whose family owned for centuries an estate on the Baltic coast, and who became one of Cecil Rhodes' pioneers in nineteenth century South Africa. The author has used aspects of an unusual family history, with links to key players in World War 2, in crafting his third novel, *A Gift of Treason*.

He spent most of his working life in the insurance industry before fulfilling an ambition to write. After his first novels, there has been a gap of thirteen years, while he devoted himself to the care of his youngest daughter, who suffered lifelong illness. After her sad death, he has returned to writing.

For Karina

A GIFT OF TREASON

MALCOLM BLAIR-ROBINSON

Other titles by this author:
Downfall
The Judas Cross

Published 2008 by arima publishing

www.arimapublishing.com

ISBN 978 1 84549 316 5

© Malcolm Blair-Robinson 2008

All rights reserved

This book is copyright. Subject to statutory exception and to provisions of relevant collective licensing agreements, no part of this publication may be reproduced, stored in a retrieval system, or transmitted in any form or by any means, without the prior written permission of the author.

Printed and bound in the United Kingdom

Typeset in Garamond 11/14

This book is sold subject to the conditions that it shall not, by way of trade or otherwise, be lent, re-sold, hired out, or otherwise circulated without the publisher's prior consent in any form of binding or cover other than that which it is published and without a similar condition including this condition being imposed on the subsequent purchaser.

In this work of fiction, the characters, places and events are either the product of the author's imagination or they are used entirely fictitiously. Any resemblance to actual persons, living or dead, is purely coincidental.

Swirl is an imprint of arima publishing.

arima publishing
ASK House, Northgate Avenue
Bury St Edmunds, Suffolk IP32 6BB
t: (+44) 01284 700321

www.arimapublishing.com

CHAPTER ONE

Normally she would have noticed it at once. But today the paper was late because the boy was ill and a friend had doubled up. Thus the post arrived first. When the boy put the newspaper on the little oak seat in the porch, it covered the letter.

As she reached the bottom of the stairs that morning, Jane looked through the clear glass panels of the front door and saw the paper there. This was a broadsheet of liberal views. It was her habit never to look at it before breakfast, unlike the post, which she always opened right away. Now it appeared there was no post, so she turned in the little hall and made her way to the kitchen at the end of the short passage. Everything was laid out ready from the night before. The tea was in the pot and the kettle was full, ready to be switched on. All she needed to do was to pop a slice of toast into the toaster and shake some flakes into the bowl. She liked the sort with dried fruits.

As she crunched away at the cereal and sipped tea she considered her programme for the day. It was Friday. That meant a visit to the shops. She always bought her provisions in Harvestdown. The village was large enough, some people thought of it as a small town, to support several shops and a post office. Although savings could be made at one of the giant supermarkets, the nearest was twelve miles away and the economies available on a shopping list for one hardly justified the effort.

Shopping was important to Jane. She was not a health freak but she believed in eating healthy food. Fresh meat and vegetables. Sometimes she baked her own bread. The ten years spent nursing her mother through onsets and remissions of cancer had taught her that care of the body lightened the burden on the soul. Her mother had been completely uninterested in cooking and practiced the skill at the most primitive level, packets mostly, or tins. She smoked like a chimney. In her younger days she probably drank a good deal. Although she hated it, Jane reflected that it was just as well her mother sent her to boarding school when she was very young and kept her there until she left to go to art school. At least she was properly fed during the term time. School food, though unexciting, was good for you. Better, anyway, than the tins.

Jane looked up at the clock on the wall. It was twenty-five past eight. She was on schedule. This was important to her. She was one of the relatively few lucky people whose lives were ordered entirely independently of anybody else's. Jane recognised that this could lead to degeneration and disorder, so she had established her own exacting routine. Her alarm went off at 8 am. After waking she would always dress. There was no wandering around the house in a dressing gown. As today was shopping day, she wore her chunky sweater, plaid skirt, she could not now remember whether she had chosen Macleod or Macdonald but she liked the mix of colours, navy stockings and sensible shoes. She never had to waste time putting on make-up because she never wore any, save for a little lipstick which hardly took a moment. Her dark hair had natural waves. When she was a small child the curls had been quite tight, so it required very little attention except cutting to keep it the right length. This she did herself.

She rarely looked in the mirror. When she did so she saw an oval face with straight pointed nose and chin, brown eyes, a slightly darker shade than her hair, and perfect teeth. Her mother had been very fussy about teeth. Jane still used the same dentist in Wimpole Street. She was entirely without personal vanity and thought her image *sensible*, rather like her shoes. Others thought her looks had considerable potential, men especially. This did not interest Jane. She had no experience of men, although she was not quite a virgin. There had been this rather handsome boy in her last year at school. He was a grammar school pupil who lived in the village that surrounded her school grounds. Consorting with boys was an offence so grave that the normal punishment was expulsion.

A healthy shot of rebellion coursed through the young Jane's veins and the two used to meet in the woods. Innocently at first, then the lad became more demanding. Sex education was an unheard of vulgarity at Pickards even in the late sixties, and the girls had to make do with biology lessons concerned with the breeding habits of mice, rabbits and other small mammals. After that it was up to their imaginations. This learning process clearly had its shortcomings and Jane had not understood what was happening until it was too late. There had been no pleasure, but quite a lot of pain. Fortunately they had to separate almost immediately at the sound of approaching voices, so the nightmare of a pregnancy was avoided. The experience had served to convince Jane that sex had no useful part to play in her life thereafter. Even now in her mid-thirties, her thoughts had not changed on the matter.

Jane set off immediately after breakfast. There was no time to look at the newspaper, so it remained on the seat in the porch. The 2CV started first go. With a racket that fell far short of mechanical refinement, she backed out of the garage and down the little drive, which ran beside the house into the street. The Hollies was the last property in the village. The built-up area adjoined it to the west, but to the east it was bordered by fields and woods. A Victorian single-fronted detached villa, its name conjured in the imagination exactly the reality. A bay window with up and down sashes with the front door beside it, now with the added porch. Mellowed and friendly with just a small garden at the front, but quite a large plot at the rear. A garage, a much later edition, had been built in the garden at the back of the house, hence the rather charming little drive.

Inside, it was surprisingly spacious. Downstairs there were two good sized rooms, as well as the kitchen, and upstairs there were three bedrooms and a bathroom, although the third bedroom was really more of a boxroom. Jane's bedroom was at the back and overlooked the garden and the fields, whilst her mother's had been at the front. Jane had now turned this into her studio. The northern light was best and it was cooler in summer.

Her mother had left her the house, as well as investments, so she was of independent means provided she lived frugally. As it was, her fees for her drawings and paintings were mounting up all the time, but she continued to live carefully. This meant she was often able to invest the surplus. Jane enjoyed this. It made her feel more secure. As she often told herself, the price for living a completely independent life, free of the pressures of other people, was that in a crisis there was no one to turn to. One must be able to cope.

Jane accelerated towards the village centre with a muted roar. The rooks, disturbed by the sound, flew above the trees cawing in excitement. In the porch the newspaper sat patiently covering its secret on the oak bench.

In the distance the little car stopped and Jane went first into the butcher's. She was greeted by a "Good Morning Miss Block". After all these years it might be expected that she would be known as *Jane* throughout the village. Although she had lived there since she was five, people felt she was, well not exactly aloof, she was always friendly and willing to exchange the time of day, but perhaps distant. Private. Yes, private. People respected that it was Jane's way to keep herself to herself. Harvestdown was still an homogenous community where people understood each other. It was not pretty enough to attract weekenders, with their town ways and cash based values. People may not have felt close to Jane but the spinster artist who lived alone at the end of the village was as much a part of it as the oak planted to mark Queen Victoria's Diamond Jubilee.

Later, when Jane returned, she entered the house from the back and first put away her food. She had brewed her mid-morning coffee before she remembered the paper and her disappointment at no post. To her surprise she found the letter underneath the newspaper in the porch. Jane wondered whether this meant that the post was early or the newspaper late. It was not at all important but Jane liked to know the details of what went on around her. With a slight shrug of her shoulders she gathered the letter and the newspaper and returned to the kitchen.

Jane sat down at the table and looked at the envelope. It was a brown A4 and postmarked Winchester. She had thought it must be a circular from the district council. They sent them from time to time giving news of environmental issues. Jane usually recognised her post. She owed no money and had no credit cards. She did have a debit card which deducted payments direct from her bank account, but she used this only in an emergency which, in her predictable life, was seldom. Whenever she completed any kind of form she always ticked the box indicating that her name was not to be passed on, so she received very little junk mail. Her telephone number was ex-directory and she had not registered to vote. Her mother had never done so, apparently out of laziness, but for Jane the omission was deliberate. She considered all politicians to be liars. Some lied all the time, some part of the time, but sooner or later they all lied. She was aware that democracy was the guarantor of freedom, which she cherished, but why must freedom be based upon lies? Could it thus be truly freedom? Jane was not sure, so she judged it right, honourable even, to abstain.

As she studied the envelope she became uneasy. The address had been typed on an old-fashioned typewriter which had seen better days. What could this be? Jane did not like mysteries, even trivial ones which passed in a moment. She took a knife and slit the top so that the letter slipped out easily. She read:

12 Flower Street,
Winchester, Hants.

29 April 1988

Dear Jane
You do not know me but I am a retired literary agent. A client of mine who was also a friend of long standing entrusted me with certain property which was to be passed to your late mother, Diana Block, twenty years after his death.

That time has now come but your mother has, I know, regretfully died. My instructions were that, in such an event, this unusual bequest was to come to you. It was not part of the formally acknowledged estate of my client. The story behind it is long and complicated and will impact quite significantly upon your life.

Arthritis makes correspondence difficult now and rather than try to convey on paper what would flow much easier face to face, I would ask you to visit me here. Next Tuesday, 6th May, for a light lunch would be ideal. Arrive by noon. Though perhaps burdened by the end of it, I believe you will find the day worthwhile. No confirmation is necessary. Ring to rearrange, but I hope not. The house is easy to find, very close to the town centre.

To help set the scene I enclose a small photograph.

Yours sincerely
Harold W. G. Trubshaw

Jane looked inside the envelope and found the photograph. It was a black and white snapshot of her mother, youthful, wearing a sweater, knee breeches and what looked like heavy boots. She was sitting on the porch of some sort of house or cottage, but the property was not shown as the photographer had stood, for a snapshot anyway, quite close. Beside her mother stood a lean, not unattractive man with dark hair, maybe a year or two older and similarly dressed. To their right was a cluster of pot plants in a shallow box standing on some bricks at each end. Behind was the closed door of the property. The major feature was fixed above the door. It was a pair of antlers. On the back was written, not in her mother's hand, *August '49*.

Although as she looked at the man there was to Jane a vague familiarity, it was not her father. The writing on the back was not his either, but maybe he had taken the picture. This was of good quality, Jane could tell. In connection with her work she was quite a proficient photographer and she could recognise the output of a quality camera. Jane looked at the address on the envelope which was, as the postmark indicated, in Winchester. What on earth could this mean? A bequest to her mother from twenty years ago! Outside the deceased's formal estate? Impact quite significantly on her life? Perhaps burdened? Jane read the letter again. There was a telephone number. She would ring. She stood up to reach the telephone mounted on the kitchen wall behind her chair and was about to dial when she stopped, her finger hovering uncertainly in the air. Would it not be better to wait? Today was Friday. It was only till Tuesday. Not long. Manageable. Just.

Jane sat down again. She picked up the photograph. Who was this man? A friend or relative? She knew what she should be thinking, but her mind would not wrap itself around the word *lover*. Not that she cared much whether her mother had a lover in the past. She could have had several. Jane worried solely of the effect on her father. Although only four when he died, she was devoted to him. She had carried that devotion throughout her childhood and into adult life and, with a passion normally felt only for the living, she was devoted to him still. Suddenly, in the form of an enigmatic letter in a scruffy envelope, Jane felt, moreover *she knew*, that her life, so ordered, predictable and self-managed had received a jolt. How severe she could not yet tell. She would have to take a firm grip to retain control. Yes, she must not lose control. She sipped her coffee. It was now lukewarm. She moved across the kitchen and threw it down the sink. She did not pour another.

That afternoon Jane decided on a short hike to the Downs. The round trip would be four miles. After the shock of the morning it would help to keep her occupied. She was working on paintings for a calendar which had been commissioned by an office equipment manufacturer who wished to enhance its image by avoiding scantily clad girls on its offering for the following year. The advertising people had come up with the idea of wild flowers for each month of the year. Jane's reputation brought her the job.

For the month of May she had chosen *salad burnet*. It was of the rose family and could be found on chalky grassland between April and August. The leaves smelled of cucumber when crushed and had been popular for use in medieval salads. Although the tiny flowers were green and without petals, they had bright yellow stamens and tall red styles, which made the appearance unusual. Jane was very particular about her paintings, and although she might produce the same flower in different situations, she liked always to sketch and photograph an authentic setting each time. Thus she could develop and embellish in her studio what was an actual sighting.

Earlier, after her aborted morning coffee, Jane had gone upstairs to her studio to work, but instead found herself staring out the window and thinking of her father. Her recollection was of a kind, gentle but frail man whose evident affection for her mother was mostly rebuffed by the chillier self-centred personality of Diana. There was certainly an underlying passion of which Jane herself was the evidence, but towards the end of her father's life such moments were few. Robert Block suffered from a congenital weakness of the heart which grew worse in early middle age and became critical as he approached fifty. By then he had given up working in the City, it was said "in tea" but even now Jane was not quite sure what this meant, and remained at home while her mother worked as a civil servant in Whitehall.

Thus it was that the toddler Jane came to rely on her father as the dominant parent in her life. In the mornings, if she awoke early, she would go into her parents' room and snuggle up to him on his side of the bed. On that morning she had found him cold with his eyes half open and strange. After a while she had crawled across him and awakened her mother. Diana's exclamation of "Oh God!" had echoed in Jane's memory down through the years, but as she grew older she came to realise it had been a cry not of despair, grief, fear or even helplessness, but rather one of annoyance.

In the end things had not turned out so badly. There had been a little capital in the background and some quite significant life insurance bought years earlier by her father at youthful rates before health clouds loomed. Her mother sold the suburban house they owned in expensive Bromley and bought The Hollies for less than a third of the proceeds. On the grounds of widowhood and responsibility for her child Diana had then retired, in those now far-off days when caring for one's own children was considered a worthwhile contribution to society, not to be contracted out to inexperienced teenagers.

Unfortunately Diana was next to useless at these family chores and by the time Jane was eight she was at boarding school. She did not mind the long absences from home. Her affection for her mother was at a minimalist filial level. Her admiration for her father had not diminished and as the little girl believed that in some mystical way he was still near her, this comfort was as real in the sparse and draughty school dormitory as it was in the relative comfort of the home fireside.

After his death her mother spoke little of Jane's father. Towards the end, Diana Block's emaciated form sat huddled in the armchair in the corner of her bedroom, her sunken eyes, wheezing breath and hacking cough witness to years of self-abuse by alcohol and tobacco. With her body now racked by invading cancer, she muttered once or twice to Jane, "Your father and I had some good times together". She never specified when, so Jane could only speculate either a more relaxed lifestyle than she could remember or wishful thinking.

The clouds had dispersed and the sun was shining as she plodded up the sloping footpath towards the Downs. Carrying a strong hazel walking stick to give her confidence (a woman walking on her own was vulnerable after all), she breathed deeply on the fresh spring air. A small rucksack was slung on her back containing her sketchpad and crayons, a collapsible canvas stool of the kind used by fishermen, and her camera. This was an expensive Nikon fitted with a 24mm macro lens, as favoured by the professionals. Although Jane always worked from her sketches, she liked to compare the results afterwards with the reality. She took numerous photographs on each excursion and had a huge collection of transparencies which she could project onto the wall of her studio. They were stacked in their boxes, neatly labelled and indexed, so that she could refresh her memory in a moment by viewing the image of almost every plant she had ever painted. The rucksack also contained a light waterproof. Showers in April could be both unexpected and heavy.

High above her, larks trilled their celebration of the onset of spring as Jane strained her eyes against the sun to try and spot the tiny hovering birds. Nearer the ground there was a flash of yellow. Was it a greenfinch or a grey wagtail? Ahead of her, higher up the hill, she could see another walker. A man. He seemed to be using binoculars. Probably a bird-watcher. Later, when Jane looked again, he had disappeared.

The path took her through ancient woodland. It became quite steep before a stile brought her into a grassy meadow high on the side of the Downs. She made for a corner of the enclosure and smiled with pleasure as she saw the clump of *salad burnet* near where she had seen it last year, but this time more prolific.

Soon she was seated on her little stool sketching, having already taken several photographs from different angles. She passed the afternoon in contentment, the looming revelation about the mysterious bequest out of her mind, concentrating on the artistic flair that enabled her to transpose the supreme but perishable creation of Mother Nature to a permanent image. This could be seen and enjoyed by countless thousands not witness to the pastoral scene in the high green meadow on that April afternoon. Not witness either to the flash of reflected light caught on the lenses of powerful binoculars, trained upon the artist from the cover of the wood behind her.

CHAPTER TWO

At last it was Tuesday. Jane had managed to keep herself busy over the intervening days by concentrating on her painting. She had now reached August on the calendar, using her slide collection for inspiration. That morning Jane dressed with unaccustomed care. She knew that her host for lunch was old, but she nevertheless felt the occasion to be special. She would look her best. She even chose her finest silk underwear, although the prospect of this being revealed to the old man was well outside the scope of probabilities.

She stood in front of the full-length mirror in her bedroom in stockings and suspenders, she considered tights unhygienic, and wondered if her reflection was erotic. She supposed it must be. She had quite a good figure. Admittedly her bust was a little small and her hips a trifle wide. Her thighs, though full, were firm and her ankles and feet, like her wrists and hands, were slender and well formed. She could have cultivated an understanding of make-up, but she had never bothered. Today, however, she applied a little eyeliner as well as lipstick. She was quite pleased at the outcome.

Finally, resplendent in a red wool dress, she set off in the 2CV towards Winchester. She avoided the main roads and motorways and kept to the B-roads, cutting behind Chichester and then striking north-west towards Petersfield, but passing south of it, before crossing the Meon valley and on to Winchester.

She tried to picture the town in Jane Austen's day. Now in the late nineteen eighties many of the buildings would have changed, but some would be the same. The big difference would be in the crowds, the cars and the atmosphere. Motoring had brought mobility to everyone, but in doing so it had damaged the environment and the quality of life. Jane felt strongly about these things. The car sported a Greenpeace sticker.

She parked near the town centre and made her way on foot. Jane had arrived early so there was time to get her bearings. She called at an estate agent to locate the address. They showed her a map. It was easy. Flower Street was close to the centre above the cathedral. To pass the time, Jane sat by the river in the spring sunshine. As the bright water chortled and bubbled past her on its journey to the sea, she felt excited at the prospect of her meeting, if a little apprehensive of its tidings.

At ten to twelve she made her way up the hill and found her destination without difficulty. Spoiled only by parked cars, the little Georgian houses were much as they had ever been. Number sixteen had a well-kept air, though it was clean and cared for rather than newly painted or refurbished.

The front door knocker and doorknob were brass and highly polished. The step was well scrubbed, and the tiny front garden, bordered by a railing and not more than four paces deep, was colourful with polyanthus.

Jane studied the knocker. A ring through a lion's mouth. On the doorjamb was a small brass bell with a white porcelain button saying PRESS in black letters. The constant polishing had worn the chasing of the original metal, and the paint on the wood around it was faded. Jane chose the bell. She rang it and heard a melodious tinkling deep within. Footsteps approached. Then the door was opened by a short, stout woman of about sixty, with a pink face and white hair, wearing a flowered apron over a black dress.

Jane hesitated. "Oh, good morning. I have an appointment, well, for lunch, actually, with Mr Trubshaw. He wrote to me. I am Jane Block."

The response was not encouraging. "Oh dear me..."

Jane became anxious. "Is there something wrong?"

The short lady looked past Jane into the street and cast an anxious glance in each direction. "You had better come in," she said.

Jane was ushered along the narrow hall and into the front room. Small but charming. An impression of pictures and chintz.

Behind her the woman spoke again. "Mr Trubshaw is dead."

Jane swung round in disbelief. "Dead? But he only sent me... I mean, I had this letter only, only on Friday!"

The woman shook her head. "I did not know. Otherwise I would have been in touch."

"Was it very sudden?"

"Oh indeed, yes. There was a break-in on Thursday night. He woke up to find a burglar rummaging through the papers on his desk in his bedroom. He shouted and the man escaped through the window, down the drainpipe, or maybe he jumped, it's not very high. The shock was too much. Mr Trubshaw's heart was none too good, and the next day, Friday, it stopped, just when the police had left after taking the details. About mid-morning. I was in the kitchen. I heard the crash as he fell off the chair in the dining room where he had gone with his old portable to write letters."

Jane moved forward and took the little woman by the arm, pulling her down to the sofa so that they were both seated.

"How awful for you! What a dreadful thing! Such a shock!"

Jane looked into dark blue eyes, which grew moist, though otherwise the woman remained composed.

"I'm so sorry, I should have introduced myself. I am Phyllis Tripper, Mr Trubshaw's housekeeper. My late husband used to drive the car and look after the garden when Mr Trubshaw had the house in the country at West Meon. After my husband died, Mr Trubshaw decided to sell and move here. He felt the town centre was more suitable for the elderly, and this little house is much easier for me."

"Yes, yes... Of course," murmured Jane absently. She was thinking of the letter and the promised story behind it. "Did Mr Trubshaw mention me to you at all?"

"No, I'm afraid he didn't, but he never discussed his business affairs with me." Mrs Tripper looked at Jane. "Are you one of his authors?"

"No." Jane hesitated. "Mr Trubshaw wrote to me about a bequest to my mother from a client of his. As my mother died a few years ago, Mr Trubshaw wished to talk to me."

"Oh, that explains it. I thought you were rather young. Mr Trubshaw had not taken on any new authors for years. He just looked after the interests of one or two old friends. Funny, I don't remember an author by the name of Block."

Jane hesitated again. "Oh I don't think he was a relative. Poor Mr Trubshaw was going to explain it all to me today." Jane reached into her handbag. She brought out the photograph and showed it to Mrs Tripper. "I suppose you don't recognise this man, do you by any chance?"

The woman squinted and held it at a distance. "Oh dear no. Quite handsome though. You mentioned a bequest. Did he die recently?"

"Well if he was the client Mr Trubshaw spoke of, he died twenty years ago."

Mrs Tripper shook her head. "That would be in 1967. We did not start to look after Mr. Trubshaw until 1970, so it was before our time". She stole an anxious glance at the clock on the mantelpiece. "I would offer you lunch, but I am just preparing to attend the funeral. His son and daughter-in-law and one or two other relatives will probably return here for tea."

Jane waved her hand. "Don't even think of it. I couldn't possibly put you to the trouble at such a time."

She was worried now. She might never solve the riddle. She stood up. "I suppose you have no knowledge of any papers connected with my late mother in Mr Trubshaw's possession?"

Mrs Tripper shook her head. "Oh dear, no. I was never involved in anything like that. I don't think he kept many papers. He had a huge bonfire before we left West Meon. He said there was no point now, and in a small house we did not want to be cluttered up."

"But you said the burglar was rummaging through papers on his desk?"

Mrs Tripper's cheeks reddened slightly. "Oh yes, you're quite right, I did. But it was just everyday correspondence. Nothing fancy or legal."

On the doorstep Jane shook Mrs Tripper's hand. "I really am so sorry."

The little woman looked up at her. "If you ask me, it was as good as murder! The doctor said it could have happened at any time, but had he not had the shock of waking to find a burglar, he would certainly be alive to have lunch with you today." She shook her head before closing the door. Jane caught the glisten of tears on her cheeks.

Standing in the street, Jane wondered what to do next. She could not recall such a let-down. Up until last Thursday everything in her life had been organised and certain, independent and free. Now suddenly she had a snapshot in her handbag and was the inheritor of some unusual and possibly burdensome legacy, which was unofficial and known only to the old man now in his coffin. An intruder in the night? Jane shivered. She felt light-headed.

She walked down the hill, across the town centre and along narrow streets around the perimeter of the cathedral. Soon she was in another world. Fine old properties, clustered together, told of ages past when communities hung close in kinship and mutual interest. Jane could feel the history. She sensed the presence of ancient scholars and men of letters. This was where the foundations of the finest education were set, upon the certainties gleaned from centuries of the pursuit of knowledge. Yet, what knowledge was this? Was this knowledge that enlightened, or knowledge that constrained? Was there within these perimeters the quest for truth, or was an earlier truth being protected and defended from the assault of newer and greater truths from outside?

Soon Jane was close to the college. Boys in tweed jackets and flannels moved this way and that, orderly and studious. Jane stood for a moment and watched. Had the man in the picture once been one of these? He looked refined. Public school probably. Her father was at Dover College. A public school, yes, but not within miles of the Winchester standard.

She felt hungry now. There was a pub on the corner. Jane hesitated. Pubs were not the sort of place for women alone. A wine bar, perhaps. Yet somehow this looked different. On impulse she pushed the door and went inside. It was spacious and friendly. A cosy fire was burning to draw the chill from old walls. Around the room were tables and chairs. There were several still free. At those occupied, the diners appeared well-to-do. Jane approached the bar nervously.

"Have you a table for one?" she enquired.

The girl was welcoming. "Any not marked reserved are free." She sensed Jane's unease at being alone. "May I get you a drink?"

"A glass of red wine, please."

"If you would like to choose something from the menu..." the girl pointed to various blackboards hanging behind the bar, "...we will bring it to your table."

Jane scanned the selection which was considerable. She chose beef casserole with green peppers. She sat at a small table by the window. Her spirits lifted by the wine, she looked out at the narrow street at the boys passing by, interspersed with tourists. All was tranquil, restrained, ordered. Manners, courtesy. These boys would go on, unlike her father who finished up "in tea", to Oxbridge, then to the civil service or politics. Contemporaries would find their paths constantly crossing until at last they held the reins of the nation. Mandarins and Ministers. The Power and the Glory.

Yet what chance awaited as sharp a brain from the decay of the inner city, the squalor of the tower block? The political meddling in the educational process led to endless argument and dispute. What did they mean when they said a classless society had arrived? Freedom? Choice? Opportunity? These were illusions surely. Jane had little real interest in politics, but suddenly sitting in the pub that day she felt ashamed. Pickards was not a centre of academic excellence, but it had good facilities for its day and saw to it that its girls did their best. Jane felt she owed all to the values by which she was, at this moment, cosily enveloped, yet had put nothing back into the vacuum of despair and neglect so frequently brought to her sitting room on television. "Well, it's not my fault" she always told herself. Yet now she wondered whether indirectly it was. Maybe not everything should be blamed on lying politicians. Perhaps it was cowardly, not honourable, to abstain.

"May I sit here?"

She looked up into a pair of dark brown eyes, set wide and deep in a square and craggy face. The pub had filled up. Jane supposed that the vacant chair at her table must be the only one free.

She nodded. "Of course," and repeated herself as no sound came from her mouth the first time.

Setting a pint of beer and a cheese ploughman's down on the little table, the stranger extended a large, well-manicured hand.

"My name is Tim Gulliver, as in the travels."

Jane responded with mounting anxiety. "Jane. Jane Block," she murmured as she took his hand.

The brown eyes twinkled. "You must forgive my approaching you directly, Jane, but these tables are too tiny to follow the English custom of pretending that the other person isn't there."

Jane had hardly been in a pub since her days at art college. Even less on her own, and never before accosted by a stranger in this way. An annoyingly good-looking one as well. She was uncertain what to do. This caused no problem to the stranger, who chatted on amiably. It turned out he was a writer of thrillers. No blockbusting bestsellers, but he made a steady living. His hobbies were photography and mountaineering.

"Not the serious stuff. Can't possibly cope with rock faces or anything like that. The best I can do is little more than exposed scrambling."

He was a frequent visitor to the Alps and had made two trips to Nepal. In the face of this biographical deluge, Jane volunteered that she was a commercial artist and an illustrator of handbooks.

"Handbooks? Really? How interesting. What sort?"

"Do you know *The Nature Lover's Guides*?"

"Certainly."

"Well, I do the flowers."

Tim's face lit up. "I always carry them in my rucksack. That's tremendous. Will you have another drink?"

Jane demurred. She doubted that he carried the guides. She was driving after all. She was not sure she should accept hospitality. Eventually she agreed to an orange juice, which she sipped carefully whilst Tim downed another beer in large appreciative gulps.

"I'm afraid it's the only way to drink it," he chuckled. "You get the full flavour."

"Oh," said Jane.

"Mind you, you can only do it with real beer. Try it with that ridiculous carbonated stuff that most people drink, and you would blow up!" He laughed out loud. Jane thought the prospect of exploding beer drinkers disgusting. He went on. "What fun we should earn our living in similar sorts of ways."

Jane agreed, but was not at all sure where this was leading. She needed to go to the Ladies, so she excused herself with the usual nose-powdering half-truth. When she returned, she saw, with some relief, that Tim Gulliver had gone. There was a scrap of paper on which he had written his telephone number and a short message.

Enjoyed meeting. My pen name is Paul Harvey. Had to dash. If you'd like to meet again, ring.

No chance of that, thought Jane, but she folded the note neatly and put it in her handbag.

Walking back to the car, Jane came to a bookshop. It was not one of the big chains. On impulse she stepped through the door. Inside was quaint, as the building was old. It was full of nooks and crannies and notices saying "Mind the step" or "Mind your head". Mostly Jane saw non-fiction, academic books and classics but there was one alcove for popular fiction. Here she found sections for romance, crime, mystery and adventure.

There did not appear to be any bestsellers and Jane had the impression that the stock reflected the taste of customers who read regularly and bought less well-known authors with a steady output, as one might expect to find in a lending library. She began in the crime section but could find nothing by Paul Harvey. In the Mystery section she had more luck. There were two titles by her new friend. Well not friend. Contact.

She chose *A Challenge in Truro - An Inspector Garlick Mystery*. Jane told herself that if one met any author, even just in passing, it was sensible, fun even, to buy one of his books. Just the one.

The woman at the pay desk had grey hair, glasses on a chain and a cashmere cardigan. Her eyes were kindly enough, though perhaps a touch wistful. Jane could tell she was a spinster. She took the book and smiled.

"Oh yes, I like him. Not one of the top selling authors customers always seem to favour nowadays, but reliable and well written. Civilised characters too, not ruffians!" She handed Jane her purchase in a neat purple bag.

Jane was thoughtful as she went on her way. Is this where I am headed, she asked herself as she watched her feet tread the uneven pavement. Fifty something, a cashmere cardigan and a wistful eye?

She walked slowly back to the car park. She wanted to talk to a friend, not a stranger in a pub, but someone close. She thought of Celia. They had been inseparable at boarding school and had stayed close friends in the years that followed. As is often the case with close friends, they were completely different. Jane envied Celia her looks. Her natural blond hair was exactly the shade that women spent fortunes at hairdressers to acquire artificially, and her open face with its huge eyes, small nose and broad mouth presented an aspect which all acknowledged to be beautiful. When she smiled with her opalescent blue eyes the effect was stunning.

Her figure, too, appeared to be without flaw. Jane had envied Celia her bigger bust, her smaller hips and her longer legs. Indeed, although Jane would never admit it, she had spent so much time in her formative years in the shadow of her apparently perfect friend, that she had come to undervalue and underestimate her own good looks and sexuality. Moreover, unable to compete with Celia, she had shut these things out of her life, telling herself that they did not exist.

Unfortunately, the blessing which Celia enjoyed, of being able to capture the heart of any man she wanted with no more effort than most people would have to apply to make a cup of tea, turned out to be rather mixed. It allowed her to treat marriage as an experiment rather than a commitment. As a result of this she was already on her fourth husband.

The two girls had been out of touch in recent years, apart from cards for Christmas and birthdays. Celia's latest marriage and the terminal illness of Jane's mother had rather coincided, so contact had been lost. That was two years ago. Jane wondered if the marriage was still intact. She had Celia's address in the little notebook in her handbag that she always carried. It was a village south of Newbury, and consequently, not very far north of Winchester.

The journey took little more than half an hour. The village was well signposted, and she found the house without difficulty because it was the biggest and impossible to miss. Jane knew a little about architecture and recognised it as Queen Anne. It was on three floors. Mellowed, perfectly proportioned and warmly inviting. Jane cut the engine and drew to a halt at the foot of the broad steps leading up to the front door.

By the time she had mounted three of the five treads, the door was thrown open and a radiant Celia, casually exotic in a loose pink cotton sweater and cream slacks, ran down the steps and embraced her with a hug of welcome that almost caused Jane to lose her balance.

"Darling, what a surprise! How wonderful!"

Before she could collect her thoughts, Jane found herself dragged by the hand up the steps, into the house, across a hall with a dangerously polished parquet floor and over-gilded antique mirrors, through French doors and out onto a patio. Celia pushed her down into a well-cushioned chair.

"Such a thrill to see you! I'm all alone. Monty... such a poppit. Have you met him? I can't remember... is in New York or somewhere on a trade mission or something. He's well on his way to the top in the Foreign Office, you know. Mind you, career does not matter to him. He's absolutely loaded. Family owns thousands of acres in Argentina. So we just use his salary for holidays and things. Wait there a second. I'll get Theresa to make us some tea."

With that, Celia disappeared back into the hall. So far, Jane had not said a single word. Shortly, Celia was back again, gushing once more.

"Let me look at you! You look radiant!" Celia's face took on a knowing look. "I know, Jane. You've met a man."

At last Jane spoke. "Oh no, really I haven't."

Celia would not be put off. "Of course you have. I can tell. And about time, too. What does he do?"

"Celia, I haven't. Well, only for half an hour, and he's a complete stranger!"

"If you have met him for half an hour he's not a stranger. What's his name?"

"Tim Gulliver."

"What does he do?"

"He's a novelist."

"Really? How exciting. Perhaps we've got one of his books in the library?"

"He writes under the name of Paul Harvey," confided Jane grudgingly.

"Oh! Not a bestseller by the sound of it. I have never heard of this Paul person. Mind you", confided Celia, " I am not what you could call well read. He's probably penniless. Lots of them are you know."

"He makes a living", murmured Jane defensively.

"Darling, a living is no good! To be any use men must be rich! Choose one of the big hitters if you want an author." Celia paused for the briefest of moments. "Still I suppose you could regard your new catch as an entry level opportunity who could lead to something better!"

At this moment, to Jane's relief, a neat, formal maid with black dress and white apron, about forty and probably Spanish, appeared with tea. Mercifully, sipping Earl Grey and eating tiny sandwiches altered the tempo and stopped Celia gushing. Gradually Jane was able to restore the fabric of their relationship. As the afternoon wore into evening and their gossiping about old times became more animated, Celia insisted that Jane stay for supper.

"Just a lobster salad. It's nice and light."

Apparently every luxury was available on tap. They ate in the kitchen which was big and modern. There were no fake Victorian cupboards or other adornments to cultivate nostalgic feelings of a homely past. Rather, Jane thought the long room was more like a research laboratory or a space station. She was careful to drink one glass of wine only, because she had a long drive ahead of her. She left just before nine, with more embraces and promises to meet again really soon.

"Jane darling, you must *not* disappear again! We have such loads in common. Especially now you have a boyfriend."

As Jane drove along the dark roads in the little car, with her handbag containing Tim Gulliver's telephone number and the book she had bought on the seat beside her, a rather troubling thought was passing through her mind. She had glanced at the novel while Celia was organising the supper with Theresa. On the back cover there was the usual biographical detail of the author, but in this case the information was sparse. It merely said that Paul Harvey, a well-established writer of mysteries, was a very private person who never gave interviews or allowed any other personal publicity. How strange that so private a person should have sat down uninvited at her table at the pub and talked so much about himself during that brief acquaintance. As she thought about this, Jane became aware that the night had grown especially dark.

Suddenly the sky was lit by a flash of lightning.

CHAPTER THREE

As Jane made her way across country back towards Harvestdown, the storm followed her. She could see the bright forks of lightning as their mighty electric charges split the night in a rippling blue ribbon from sky to earth, momentarily exposing cowering trees and huddled dwellings in an eerie hue. Above the roar of the engine she could hear the rumble of the thunder. Now and again there was a sharp crash as the bolts drew closer.

Soon it began to rain. First, great slow spots, and then a torrent. The wipers flew back and forth across the windscreen as, undaunted, the 2CV splashed on its way along roads fast becoming rivers. Now and again gusts of wind rocked it, as Jane began to wish that she had not made the excursion to see her friend. She tuned into the primitive and somewhat crackly radio fitted as an afterthought and almost inaudible in the din and soon picked up a weather forecast. Unusual weather patterns in the Bay of Biscay had produced a storm which was now crossing the South. Severe for this time of year, it would give heavy bursts of rain and sharp gusts of wind. Motorists were advised to take care.

In spite of the tensions and disappointments of the day, Jane felt comforted by her talk with Celia. It gave her confidence in her own state. Although Celia had so much that Jane had not, glamour, wealth, big house, servants, husbands who could be taken on and discarded like her wardrobe of the season's clothes, Jane could detect beneath the sparkle an undertow of unhappiness. On the other hand, Jane had a little money and could manage well so long as she was careful and, of course, she was completely independent, the programme of her life depending not on a single other human being. Above all, she did not have to worry about men. She had her career and her interests. Her life was reliable, tranquil and predictable. Whatever the mystery in which she was now involved, it was about her mother, not herself. Jane tried to put negative thoughts out of her mind. Thoughts of here she was, driving through the night in a violent storm, while on the seat beside her sat her handbag containing a mysterious old photo from the past and an up to date telephone number to temptation.

By the time Jane reached Harvestdown the storm had abated, leaving evidence of its passage in the form of deep puddles, dripping trees and small bits of debris scattered around. As she closed the garage door and looked towards the village, she realised it was in darkness. There was just the faint glow of a flickering candle from a window here and there. Electrical storms often brought power cuts in this area, so Jane was well prepared. North Sea gas had been brought into the village some years back, which meant that cooking was independent of the lights. There were plenty of candles in the cupboard, as well as an old oil lamp with mantle, tall chimney and shade, which gave restful light to read by.

It was already late, nearly eleven o'clock, and it had been a taxing day, not the usual routine by any means. Bed seemed to be the best option, so Jane made herself a hot drink of chocolate, lit the oil lamp and went up to her bedroom. Soon she was cosily propped against pillows, reading the opening chapter of *A Challenge in Truro*. It was the first time she had read a mystery involving a serial detective since devouring most of Maigret in her teens. It would help to take her mind off things before she went to sleep.

After two chapters, Jane decided it was time to try and sleep and blew out the lamp. For a time, she tossed and turned, until at last she became drowsy. Eventually she slipped into that curious state when the body relaxes into a mode of shut-down, whilst the mind goes on the rampage unfettered by reality, pulsing curious, sometimes bizarre, often frightening images through the idling mechanism of the brain.

That night Jane dreamt of a key. It was in her hand as she approached a chest. Large, ancient, studded with brass nails and covered in cobwebs. As Jane put her hand forward to insert the key into the lock, she was seized by a force and pulled back. She turned to see her mother, haggard and wide-eyed, mouthing pleas in words that Jane could not fathom. Dimly aware that this was a bad dream from which she could awake, Jane struggled to the surface of consciousness, as a swimmer fighting upwards from the deep. She found her room was bathed in moonlight. Jane rarely drew her curtains. The clouds had cleared.

Then she saw it. A figure. Looming at the foot of her bed. At once Jane was engulfed by a sensation of absolute terror. She could neither move nor cry out. The figure stood, looking down at her. It made not a sound. In the moonlight she could see dark clothing and a balaclava helmet, which apart from holes for the eyes and mouth, covered the face, giving a fiendish emphasis to the spectre. In a moment it was gone. With a convulsive lurch Jane sat up. At first she thought the vision real.

It was too late to scream. Confused, on the borderline between sleep and waking, she listened in fear of some menacing sound, but there was only the silence of the night. Though now aware she had freed herself from a nightmare, she remained frozen for several minutes while reality battled for control of her fantasies. Eventually she managed to creep to the window. The countryside was tranquil in the gentle light of a waining moon.

Jane tried the light. It came on. The lines must have been repaired. Quickly she moved throughout the little house, turning on all the lights. Everything was exactly in place. She now understood just what it must have been like for that poor old man. Why had an intruder broken in to rifle through his desk? Could it be connected with the legacy? Was Jane herself now a target? Might that nightmare become a true experience?

Jane was no drinker, but she had a bottle of brandy and a bottle of sherry, mostly for cooking and some wine. She poured herself a small brandy and drank it in one swig. It was much stronger than she expected and it made her cough and splutter. She felt the fiery liquid descend as if in a ball to her stomach, but it steadied her nerves. She sat for a while in her little kitchen, shaking. Gradually she collected her thoughts. She had no doubt she must identify the man in the photograph. In the book she had begun earlier, Inspector Garlick, a rustic sleuth who was a regular in Paul Harvey whodunits, was slow and methodical but always solved his mysteries, according to the jacket synopsis, starting only with the smallest clue. Jane had a pretty good clue. The photograph. She had read enough to know the questions the inspector would ask himself.

What else did she know? Well, her man died in 1967, twenty years after the picture was taken. There were moments when she thought she had seen the face before. Was he a relative? No. Her mother's parents were killed in the Blitz while she was a teenage evacuee in Devon. Diana was brought up by an aunt who died years ago. Her father had one brother, killed at Dunkirk, and elderly parents who died before Jane was born. There was no other family. Could he have been famous? Is that why there was a hint of recognition? How could she check?

Maybe it was the brandy or maybe it was because Jane had the natural ability to think laterally which is common to self-reliant people, but she suddenly had an idea. She thought it was a very good idea. If this man had been famous, he would have been given an obituary. So if Jane contacted one of the quality papers, interested a journalist in her story without giving too much away, it should be possible to identify the figure standing beside her mother. Indeed, if he had been well known, a good journalist might recognise him without going through a year's obituaries from the library.

Of course there was a snag. The journalist would want to write about her. That would mean publicity. Jane shuddered. But there was a compromise possible. She could embargo any article until she had unraveled the riddle. Then offer first refusal on the story. At least that would put off the day of reckoning. Give Jane time to adjust. After all, the story was not about her anyway, it was about her mother. Someone or something Diana was involved in. Not Jane. Jane only came into it because her mother was dead. All the same, she wished Harold Trubshaw had not used the word "burdensome".

Tomorrow the first thing she would do, however, would be to ring a locksmith and have proper locks fitted. The present arrangements would keep out children, but were useless against a skilled operator. The intruder may have been a phantom from her mind, but next time? Well, new locks would give her useful security.

As she tried to fall asleep again, her mind wandered back to Celia and a brief holiday they had spent together in Spain. It was before her mother's illness entered the terminal period and Jane could still get away and when Celia was between marriages, before she met Monty. They did it on the cheap because Celia was short of cash and Jane never had much to spare anyway. They bought a package for a week in a tourist hotel in Marbella.

Jane was a bit apprehensive, because she feared Celia would chase after all the men. But she had nothing to worry about. They were all "far too common", Celia explained, continuing, "I wouldn't even think of it". Jane was the opposite of a snob and always felt embarrassed about her private education. She felt this had disconnected her from real life as most people lived it. But on this occasion she was relieved that she and her friend would be able to enjoy their holiday in each other's company, without having to impress the male predators roving the beaches.

All went well until the second night when calamity overtook them in the form of a prawn salad that they had eaten at lunch. They were sharing a room with two single beds, but only one bathroom. The violent effects of this gastronomic misfortune attacked them simultaneously and required them to share intimacies which would have been unthinkable a few hours earlier. Fortunately, they made a speedy recovery during the course of the following day, after chewing tablets which Jane had wisely brought with her just in case and the rest of the holiday was a great success. After the events of that night, however, there seemed little point in returning to the usual modesties and they spent much time in each other's company in the nude, as the room lacked air conditioning and was hot.

One morning, Jane was pulling on her shorts when Celia, who was lying naked on her bed sipping orange juice, said, "Do you know, Janie, you have a beautiful bottom?"

"Oh, I think it's too big. The word I use is robust."

Celia looked at her. "The word you should use is sexy."

As Celia spoke Jane saw that she was stroking her body at a place which Jane herself had tried never to explore. She looked down at Celia, her body prone and perfect, the twin mounds of her breasts rising and falling gently with her breathing. Small wonder that men were always nearby.

Their eyes met. Momentarily they were locked. Celia spoke softly. "Will you kiss me here?"

Jane was startled. "I would rather not."

Celia smiled. "You cannot ignore your sexuality, you know. Keeping it locked away as if it didn't exist. It's part of your life, and until you let it out you will never lead your life to the full!"

"Let's go down to the beach," said Jane.

Lying now in her bed in Harvestdown and becoming gently drowsy again, Jane thought of the scrap of paper with the telephone number. Maybe she should ring this author. If he wrote mysteries he might have some ideas to help her solve hers. The contact would be strictly business of course. Sex would not come into it. Jane was soon fast asleep.

When she awoke in the morning, she was surprised to see that it was nearly half past nine. She found a locksmith in the yellow pages who agreed to treat the job as an emergency. By eleven he had arrived, and by four o'clock Jane was sitting in her kitchen drinking tea in a house that was now completely secure. Double-mortise locks and chains had been fitted to the doors, and locks had been fitted to the windows. At least silent entry would now be impossible. Jane had declined the suggestion of a burglar alarm. She feared she would always be setting it off herself, and in any event, determined intruders would know how to deal with it.

She had not yet rung the paper because the home security man had always been in earshot, but alone again now, Jane rang. She had planned the call carefully in advance, so she knew who to ask for and what to say.

At her request she was put through to "Features" and was lucky to speak to the Assistant Editor. She explained the identification problem with the snapshot and gave a highly sanitized version of the background. Nevertheless, she caught the interest of this important member of the editorial staff who sensed an intriguing skeleton in a cupboard and who promised to have a reporter call Jane back. Before twenty minutes had passed, Nick Goddard was talking to Jane about her difficulty and it was agreed that she would send the photograph by registered post to the paper straight away. There was just enough time to catch the Harvestdown sub-post office.

After that there was nothing more to be done than wait and hope. She did not have to wait long.

CHAPTER FOUR

Jane had spent the following morning restlessly, resigned to a wait of at least a week before she had any news from Nick, but shortly after twelve, he was on the line.

"Don't you know who this is?"

His tone was buoyant. Jane was about to reply in the negative. After all, that was why she had sent the photo, but Nick went on to answer his own question.

"It's a young Lucian Feyrbaeme". He pronounced it *fair beam*. "He died twenty years ago. Surely you've heard of him?"

Jane stopped herself saying she was only in her teens when he died since she detected Nick was younger than she was. She racked her brains. Lucian Feyrbaeme? Memory stirred. "Wasn't he on television?"

"Among many things, yes. Look, I'm posting you his obituary which gives a fair summary of his life, together with some useful cuttings about his death."

"His death?"

Nick was clearly excited. "Yes, he was drowned on a fishing trip off the Cornish coast. Officially it was an accident, but there were rumours of foul play. No evidence. The coroner recorded accidental death. There was a gruesome aspect."

"Gruesome?"

"Yes. Body found in pieces. Ship's propeller probably. Identified by his widow."

Widow? Jane had no time to be repelled by the dismembered body. This could be a lead.

"Is the widow still alive?"

"Yes. Mitzi. Still lives in Cambridge. I've checked. Listen, I'll post all this stuff and ring me when you're ready to talk. We would definitely want to follow up any news about him. One of the most controversial characters of the post war period. Must dash. Editorial conference!"

Before Jane could say goodbye he was gone. She hung up, then lifted the phone again and dialled directory enquiries. What name did he say? Mitzi?

"Only one Feyrbaeme", the operator spelled out the name, "in Cambridge. A Mrs M."

Jane was exhilarated. In a moment she was clutching the number scribbled on the corner of the morning paper. What should she do now? Ring? "Oh hello, you don't know me but I have found a photograph of your husband with my mother and I would like to talk about it?" No, that was not a good plan. The widow might easily hang up, thinking it was a blackmail attempt or something.

The best way would be to make a visit. It would mean a quick introduction on the doorstep, but when Mrs Feyrbaeme saw how harmless Jane was, she would almost certainly invite her in. Well let's hope so!

Jane went up to her study to look at a road atlas she kept there. Cambridge was quite a distance. She would need to stay the night. Stay the night! That would be an adventure but why not? Jane looked in the AA book. She had no other accommodation list, but it was good enough. She rang a two star hotel near the centre and booked a room without difficulty. She would pay the extra to have a double for single occupancy. That way she would have her own bathroom. A worthwhile touch of luxury.

With some enthusiasm Jane spent the day preparing for her journey. She worked out a route, filled the car with petrol and checked the oil. It was a blessing that it was air-cooled. It may be noisy but there was none of that water and anti-freeze business. She packed a small bag containing clean undies and a nightie. She would not take a second outfit. That would be silly, just for one night. She would leave very early so as to try and arrive by lunchtime. Jane would have to wait for the post of course, but usually the postman was at The Hollies soon after seven. She could read the cuttings over lunch at a café after she reached Cambridge.

Next morning all went according to plan. The postman arrived with the cuttings from Nick and Jane was on her way through the village by quarter to eight. There were few people about. It would be another twenty minutes before the bustle began.

Jane made her way across country towards the M23. It took longer than she expected. Her car was safe for overtaking only if clear road stretched to the horizon, which was rarely the case. She seemed to travel a lot of miles behind lorries moving cattle or produce. When she finally reached the motorway, it was busier than she remembered. She had to keep in the slow lane and most of the time was boxed in by lorries on three sides. She was amazed that such huge vehicles could travel at such speeds. Jane was acutely aware that her little car was the obstacle they were overtaking, and no sooner had one passed, creating turbulence which made it rock on its springs, than another would loom up in the mirror. Jane clutched the wheel white-knuckled and fearful, comforting herself with the thought that if anything went wrong, she would be crushed to pulp between these titans within seconds and would know nothing of it.

As she passed through northern Essex and into southern Cambridgeshire, the countryside opened out and the traffic began to thin a little. At last she was off the motorway and across the stretch of flat country to the town of Cambridge itself. Entering from this direction there was little to hint to the proximity of one of the world's greatest seats of learning.

Jane stopped at a filling station to buy a street map. She found a local directory at a payphone which gave her Mitzi's address. The pre-war block of flats near the Fen Causeway could not be missed. It was a good position, overlooking Sheep's Green, yet still on the outskirts.

It was now midday and Jane was famished. The ritual bowl of flakes had not been equal to the demands of the day's outing. Jane decided it would be wise to park and find something to eat, then make her call after lunch. Three o'clock would be best. If the old lady was not at home, she could try later. Soon Jane was settled in a café not far from the station. The street, which would take her right to the city centre in a short walk, seemed to be full of bicycle shops and letting agencies. Jane had imagined that she might feel intimidated eating when surrounded by academics, but people at the other tables seemed quite ordinary.

She opened the envelope from *The Sentinel* and read the obituary. Lucian Feyrbaeme had enjoyed two careers, it seemed. The first had been at the Home Office as a civil servant with MI5 connections during the war. Such was his academic brilliance; he won a First in Classics at King's Cambridge. It was thought he might return as a don after the war but he stayed with the civil service, destined for the top. He began to write and his biographies of Victorian adventurers were so successful that he wanted to turn his talents to commentaries on living personalities. To give himself the freedom to do this he gave up his career and concentrated on writing full time.

Shortly after, he appeared on television as a luminary whose opinion was sought over some historical issue. His natural ease in front of the camera led to several more appearances. These in turn led him to conduct some interviews of his own. He ended up with his own programme, *The Political Question*, in which his cunning cross-examination of leading politicians became compulsive viewing with peak ratings. In spite of the risks, both ministers and opposition leaders queued to appear, though when they did so it was with dry mouths and knotted bowels.

Jane reflected upon this imposing companion beside her mother in the doorway. A political commentator? How on earth could he be connected to Diana? She checked the obituary again. Broadcasting did not begin until the Sixties. That could explain it. The picture was taken in 1949, before he became famous. Jane could not see her mother spending time in the company of anyone involved in public affairs as much as Lucian appeared to have been. Mind you, she still did not know what the connection between these two actually was.

At the moment the papers were full of talk of an imminent cabinet reshuffle. Jane took little interest in politics, so she cared not which minister was in charge of what. She had never been able to understand the concept which suggested that if a minister were inadequate at the Foreign Office, he would be capable at the Treasury. Either he was capable, surely, or he was not. The Ministry would make little difference. It seemed strange that democracy required that the nation should be governed by a kind of musical chairs. When the music of praise stopped ringing in the ears of the Prime Minister, some unfortunates would find they had nowhere to sit, but the cronies and toadies and those too threatening to trifle with would remain, but on different chairs. Jane wondered whether this process guaranteed government by the best people or the worst.

The cuttings on Lucian's death were much as Nick had described. He had set off with a companion for an inshore fishing trip from Falmouth and had never returned. The upturned boat was later found by the coastguard, with no sign of the fishermen. The weather, though squally, had been quite manageable for anyone with experience, as Lucian. For some time no bodies were found. Eventually, bits of Lucian were picked up, but of the mysterious companion there was no trace. This led to rumours that all was not as it seemed. In the end, because of lack of evidence to the contrary, a verdict of accidental death was recorded. Strangely, not only was there nothing found of the other man, but nobody knew who he was and no one answering his description was ever reported missing. A rather sinister ending, thought Jane with a shiver.

She had now read enough to give her confidence when, indeed if, she met Lucian's widow. Jane had decided to come clean and tell exactly what had happened and why she was calling. Lucian had been dead twenty years and the snapshot was forty years old, so there was little risk of anything shocking.

After her meal, Jane strolled towards the city centre. She walked down Trumpington Street and stood before one of the great pinnacles of academia, King's College. She followed the public paths, the fine gravel of which scrunched softly as she walked self-consciously past the ancient buildings overlooking vast acres of perfect lawns. She felt an echo of Winchester. She asked herself the same question again. Was this an ultimate seat of learning, or was it dedicated to the preservation of old wisdom, which denied the discovery of new truths?

She mingled with students in King's Parade, who in turn were jostled by tourists. Were these young minds being broadened and enriched, or shackled by the stuffiness of an outdated culture? She peered in the windows of the shops. There appeared a proliferation of outfitters, the smartest ones, whose small network of branches was carefully placed at the key points on the road to establishment glory. Jane looked at her watch. It was time to make her way to Cheddleton Court.

Promptly at three o'clock, Jane approached Flat 9 and rang the doorbell. She waited, nervous, for sounds from within. She heard footsteps. The door was opened a few inches then held by a chain. She could see a three-inch width of elderly face, but not much more. The light was not good.

Jane began, "Mrs Feyrbaeme? I'm awfully sorry to drop in without warning, but I was passing nearby."

The door closed immediately. Jane was momentarily dismayed until she heard the chain being drawn back from its socket. Then the door was opened wide. Before her stood a bright, sparkling woman in her late sixties, somewhat shorter than Jane, very slightly stooped with grey hair, not white, cut in a page-boy bob, probably the unchanged style of a lifetime. She wore a black wool skirt with grey blouse, over which hung a huge embroidered cardigan, a mixture of maroon, mauve and green with gilded thread here and there to give emphasis to flowers and leaves. A long amber necklace dangled from her neck, and a cameo brooch fastened the centre of her collar matching, as Jane later noticed, a ring worn on the third finger of her right hand. Her face, though covered in wrinkles and lines, was still very pretty. Blue eyes danced with enthusiasm and interest. The old lady held out her hand and pulled Jane across the threshold.

"Jane! My dear! We meet at last. I knew sooner or later you would come."

Jane was completely taken aback. She hardly knew what to say. "But Mrs Feyrbaeme, how did you know?"

Jane's question went unanswered, but the enthusiasm for her arrival continued.

"None of this Mrs Feyrbaeme. You must call me Mitzi. I was sure you would be in touch this year! It's twenty years, you know, and of course by now you have the envelope."

"The envelope?"

Jane was now totally confused. She followed Mitzi Feyrbaeme through a narrow hall into a surprisingly large living room divided by a centre arch, with a dining table at one end and twin sofas and small easy chairs at the other. The hall had been dark, but this room was bright, having windows on three sides. The furnishing was rather nineteen fifties, but the overwhelming impression was of books. They were everywhere. All around the walls were shelves. There seemed to be hundreds if not thousands of books. Some were old, leather-bound editions of the classics or earlier, others more contemporary. Where there was a gap between shelves the spaces were filled with pictures. As far as Jane could tell with a quick glance, almost all of these were sketches and cartoons of famous figures. She recognised several musicians and writers. She thought some of the others were politicians.

Mitzi guided her to a sofa and sat down beside her. "Let me look at you! I have waited so long for this moment, but I determined as soon as your mother died that I would not intrude on your life. I would wait for you to come to me. Often I thought you might never do so, but now, here you are!"

Jane's confusion mounted. After all, she had doubted that Mitzi would even see her.

"Mitzi, I had no idea that I would receive this welcome from you. I didn't even know if you would see me at all." Jane hesitated as the sparkling blue eyes regarded her intently. "Actually, I am astonished that you even know of my existence."

"Ah!" said Mitzi, throwing her hands in the air. "You poor soul. There must be so many muddles in your mind, but now," she brought her hands down on her own knees in an excited and purposeful slap, "now, you can learn the truth. First we must make ourselves comfortable. You will want to powder your nose after your journey. The bathroom is in the hall on the left. I will make some coffee." Mitzi was already on her way towards a door at the far end of the room. "I'm afraid I have no tea. It is an English habit which I was never able to acquire. I was born in Germany, you know."

Strange. Jane had caught no accent. She made her way to the bathroom. There were more books here, travel and biographies, supposedly for guests who liked to linger. Jane combed her hair and put on some lipstick. She was impressed by the care that Mitzi took of her appearance. The result was bohemian rather than glamorous, but she conveyed an instant impression of somebody who made the best of everything, including herself. She rummaged in her handbag for a compact. Had she remembered to bring it? Yes, here it was. Jane's fingers touched the paper with the phone number. She felt a sudden thrill. She applied a little powder and lipstick. As she did so her mind was in the Winchester pub.

Back in the sitting room, she just had time to look between the heavy velvet curtains at the view of Sheep's Green, when she heard the chink of fine china, and turning, saw Mitzi advancing with the coffee on a tray. They sat together on the sofa once more. Jane wanted to steer the conversation away from herself while she absorbed this unexpected environment. Her attempt lacked originality.

"I know one should not say this," said Jane, "but these are beautiful cups."

"Rockingham. A wedding present from one of Lucian's many aunts. I broke one the day they told me of his death. I knew it was a bad omen, and sure enough, when the bell rang, there was this man with a policewoman beside him. I knew."

"How awful! I know little about his death."

"We'll come to that in good time. Let me begin at the beginning."

It was quite a story. Mitzi had already mentioned she was born in Germany. Her father, a physicist, had come over to Cambridge in 1930 to take up a research fellowship that was to last three years. He had no Jewish connections, but he was passionately anti-Nazi. By the time the temporary appointment ended, Hitler and the Nazis were in control, so he applied to stay. Friends helped, and eventually he and his wife were granted political asylum. Mitzi, who was ten when they arrived, completed her schooling in England, and then went on to Girton College, where she gained a First in European History. During this period she met Lucian, who was regarded as one of the brightest minds of his generation. They became inseparable companions and finally married in 1946.

"I say inseparable companions, dear, but we were, of course, separated often. Neither of us went into uniform during the war, but because of my background, I was put into the Secret Service at its country headquarters at Wanborough, where I was a Political Warfare Officer. Lucian was sent to the Home Office. Actually, to MI5."

Jane knew nothing about the secret intelligence world. "Does that mean he was a spy?"

"Not exactly, dear, no. MI5 looks after home security. It was his job to seek out the enemy spies in our midst. When the war was over I returned to Cambridge, but he stayed at the Home Office, but not in MI5. In the end he gave it up to write full time, and then, of course, his broadcasting career developed."

Jane was in a hurry to reach the part of the story which involved her mother. She tried to hide her impatience. "Did he maintain his connections with MI5?" she asked. "In the few spy thrillers I have read people always seem to be involved even after they left!"

The sparkling blue eyes grew serious. "That's a very good point. I gave it all up, certainly. My thing was shut down anyway when the war ended. But I'm not too sure about Lucian. I think he may have maintained connections."

Jane hesitated. Her next question hovered in the murk of embarrassment, but she had to know.

"I know this may be awkward," she said at length, "but what was the connection with my mother?"

Mitzi laughed. No, it was not at all awkward. The truth was not at all what she would expect.

"I believe Lucian and I had a near perfect marriage, but the physical side, which seems to be the only thing that counts these days, well, there was very little of that. Unfortunately, I was not quite right in that department. We tried an operation, but it did not help. There was always a great deal of discomfort and little pleasure. I realised how unfair this was for a healthy man, so I told your father that I would look after his mind, but he would have to find somebody else to look after his body. Which was in his case, after all, just a shelter for his mind. Some people, you must understand, dear, have very little intellect, and so their bodies are everything to them. But Lucian's intellect was gigantic."

Jane was not quite sure about this. She, too, shared a lack of interest in her body, but in her case it did go with a gigantic intellect.

"Anyway, he eventually met your mother, I am not certain where. In London, I think. Probably a bar or something, and they became lovers. I was delighted, because from all I gathered she hardly had a brain to her head. I'm sorry, my dear," Mitzi laid a comforting hand on Jane's knee, "it's awful of me to speak of your mother in this way, but I am trying to describe to you my own feelings."

Jane nodded. Her own opinion of her mother was much the same. That was awful, too.

"Eventually our lives settled into a pattern. Lucian spent six weeks of every summer with your mother, whilst I followed my hobby, almost an obsession, I fear, of archaeology. He went off to his love nest and I went off to whatever digs the Archaeological Society was involved in. Frequently to the Middle East."

"Where did they go?"

"Actually, I have no idea. Although we had no secrets, we thought it best not to discuss the details, so I never knew where he went. I think it was to the North. I'm sure it was not a beach resort. Lucian hated such places. He always returned with a tan on his face, arms and legs, but his body was lily white as always. The tan had that northern bronze rather than the southern yellow, which I tended to pick up on my expeditions!"

Jane was beginning to tear apart inside. "What about my father?"

Mitzi frowned. "Your father, dear? How do you mean?"

"Well," said Jane, fighting back tears, "How did he feel? Did he know?"

Mitzi gripped Jane's arm. "Oh my dear! How clumsy. I can see I have upset you. And with no need! You see, all this was before your parents were married. Your poor mother could see no future with Lucian. Quite rightly. Then she met your father, Robert, wasn't it? Yes, well, it was a bit of a whirlwind that took Lucian by surprise, but he was philosophical and they parted on good terms."

Jane's mind was struggling to comprehend. Whirlwind? Or bluff called? She dared not think.

"Did my mother and Lucian meet again?"

"Only in the very occasional, formal sense. The physical relationship, the annual holidays and all the other aspects of their escapist life finished with Diana's marriage. Lucian was rather old-fashioned in many ways. He did not see himself as an adulterer because I knew everything – too much sometimes – but he did not want to ruin Diana's married life. Especially with your father's weak heart. Poor man."

Jane was not attracted to these revelations. Yet, sitting there in that flat in Cambridge, she found herself drawn to this sparkling female academic, in whom she detected a zest for life and a sense of fun that had been completely absent in her own experience with her mother. She also recognised that she was talking of events that had taken place almost forty years ago, and not only the people, but the times were different. She felt, too, that Mitzi knew rather more than she had admitted to so far.

"When I came in, you mentioned an envelope."

"Yes, have you got it?"

"Well not an envelope exactly. A letter and a photograph."

She handed them both to Mitzi, who read the letter then studied the snapshot.

"How peculiar. Mind you, I have always thought Harold was peculiar. Such an eccentric, but he did a very good job in promoting Lucian. What did he say when you met him?"

"That's the point," said Jane, "he's dead. He died before I could see him."

Mitzi's hands flew up to her face. Her eyes were wide with dismay. "No! Was it sudden, or was he ill?"

"Yes to both. He had heart trouble, but he had woken to find an intruder in his bedroom, a burglar apparently, rifling through his papers. The shock was too much and he died the next day. It was after he had sent me the letter but before I went to see him."

Mitzi shook her head. "This is very bad, very bad indeed."

Jane was startled at her change of mood. She sought to reassure. "I think it was just unfortunate. Burglaries are so common nowadays. Especially with the elderly, and his heart was frail." She went on. "It just left me rather in the lurch, which is why I came to see you. I thought you might be able to help. I never dreamt you were expecting me."

Mitzi looked up at her sharply. "Lucian's Will provided that he left everything to me except for an envelope, sealed literally with sealing wax, which was put in the care of his executor, Harold Trubshaw, to be given to your mother twenty years after his death. At first, I thought it was really just mementos of their love life. Then when I heard he had separately instructed that silly Harold to give it to you if your mother died earlier, I began to wonder. Now I am quite anxious."

"What about?"

Mitzi leaned forward. "Can you stay the night? You've got such a long journey to make and I don't like to keep you, but we need time to talk!"

Jane explained about her hotel.

"Oh, but you should have stayed here!"

"Well, I wasn't sure," Jane hesitated, "and I'm booked in now, anyway."

Mitzi brightened. "Let's go out to dinner and I will tell you the rest. I will book a table at the Riverside. It's a modern hotel overlooking the river. It's expensive, but we'll get a good meal. It will be my treat. What you need now, Jane dear, is a break."

She glanced at the clock. It was nearly six. "Let us meet there in the Lounge Bar at eight. We shall be quite comfortable. Women on their own can feel safe in this city."

Jane hesitated. "Well, I haven't brought anything to change into."

"Don't be silly, dear, you look wonderful. Anyway, this is Cambridge, not Cannes!"

So it was settled. Jane set off back to her hotel. She would freshen up and try to digest all she had learned so far. The second instalment was to come.

This would prove to be more sinister.

CHAPTER FIVE

There was plenty of time, so Jane was in no hurry to return to her room. She walked along the riverbank in the evening sunshine. It was surprisingly warm. She identified the Riverside Hotel for later on and watched the tranquil, timeless scene of the gently flowing river, the strollers on its bank and the occasional punt surging silently forward with each measured push of the pole.

Yet the delights of the eye hardly penetrated her mind, which was working feverishly to absorb the new dimension which Mitzi's revelations had given to her existence. Life was easier when it was simple. Now she was caught up in a mystery which made Mitzi anxious. Yet might this not be good for her? Already she had made the longest car journey of her life and had met this engaging old lady. Was fate taking a hand to jog her complacence? Because, she had better face it, she was complacent. Well, perhaps satisfied was a kinder word.

But was her life a success? Was she completely self-contained? Or was she in a survival mode, cut off from contact? She had no relatives living and only one friend. Dear though Celia was to her, the contact was rather haphazard and was only close when Celia was between husbands. During the marriages, Jane had to make do on her own. There was her life as a wild flower illustrator ordered into its neat and predictable routines, receiving commissions through the post and payment by credit transfer to her bank. Was this a real living life or a fossilised retreat from a real world in which she was too frightened to engage?

Back in her room, Jane took a cool shower. It was refreshing and different. She had no shower at home, but her large old-fashioned bath, an imposing affair with feet, was good to dream in. The shower, on the other hand, woke her up and sharpened her perceptions. This was what was needed, to draw the most from her dinner with Mitzi.

It was just after eight when she entered the Lounge Bar of the Riverside Hotel. Jane had hung back because she was a little nervous of arriving first. She had suffered a moment of depression as she conceded to this. Soon approaching forty, nervous at entering a smart hotel and, well, never having known a man.

Her spirits lifted as she saw Mitzi by the window. So full of zest and interest. Jane felt instinctively that Mitzi was good for her. They embraced again, even though their separation was hardly two hours. Mitzi had not changed her outfit, but Jane suspected that this was as a courtesy to herself. There had been one or two adjustments to the jewellery. The amber necklace had given way to something similar in jade, and the cameo ring and brooch were replaced by a combination of diamonds and rubies, which reflected jagged shafts of light, in confirmation that they were the real thing.

"Tell me, dear," began Mitzi, "are you driving?"

"No, I walked. It's not far."

"In that case, let's begin with cocktails." Mitzi clapped her hands in excitement.

"Cocktails?" Jane was not quite sure. She knew nothing about them. She decided to be frank.

"I know so little about cocktails. About the only one I've heard of is a dry martini."

Mitzi waved a hand. "Oh no, dear. That's much too pre-war. We'll have two margaritas! Leave it all to me. It will start our evening with a zing."

A hovering waiter, sensing that a decision had been made, approached. The order was placed, and soon Jane found herself sipping from a funnel-shaped glass, the rim of which had been dipped in salt, a liquid unlike anything she had tasted before. There was certainly plenty of *zing*, but this was not unwelcome. She was beginning to enjoy herself. Mitzi was leaning towards her.

"Tell me, dear, have you travelled much?"

Jane felt foolish. She thought it best to come clean. "No, it's awful, isn't it? Hardly anywhere, just a couple of trips to Spain, and a weekend in Paris when I was a teenager in a school party."

Mitzi clapped her hands again with pleasure. Jane found the little mannerism engaging.

"What fun! I was hoping you would say that. You see, now that I'm older," the sparkling Mitzi leant forward again, "but remember, dear, by no means old, I have given up the longer journeys because for those one needs a companion and all my contemporaries have become lazy and overweight. I could show you some of the great sights of the world. Let's plan a trip!" She thought for a moment. "I know, let's go to the Pyramids!"

"The Pyramids! Good gracious, I have never even imagined..."

Mitzi cut her short. "You will enjoy every minute. I'll arrange it all. I will speak to my travel agent in the morning. We must go before the end of May or else it will get too hot if you're not used to it."

Jane felt she had to mention something. "Mitzi, I'm not sure I can afford any big expense."

"Don't be silly, there is nothing to pay. I don't spend anything like my income. All the investments and Lucian's royalties and so on."

Jane was not sure that she should accept all this hospitality from Mitzi, but realised it was useless to argue. Anyway, it sounded too exciting. Mitzi asked about dates. Jane was able to answer that she was free at any time. At least her solitary life had that advantage.

With the meal ordered, they found themselves at a window table overlooking the garden. They had both decided on fish. Mitzi chose a light Bordeaux. The restaurant was not full, but there were enough tables occupied to make it seem busy without ruining the service. At one or two tables there were larger parties, attendees at seminars run by computer companies or similar. In the corners here and there were quieter more studious guests, academics probably, the higher levels who could afford the prices.

Suddenly Mitzi exclaimed, "Oh look, there are Inspector Jefferson and Sergeant Bramley!"

Jane turned to see a bald man and a florid companion sitting two tables away. "Inspector Jefferson? Sergeant..."

"You know, dear, the television series. Sunday evenings. You get the complete story in a single episode. The murder and the solution. Everybody is always a gentleman or a lady except poor old Sergeant Bramley. The whole thing is nonsense but I love every minute!"

Jane marvelled at Mitzi's ability to enjoy a trivial television series, when surrounded by all those books and steeped in a life of academia.

Mitzi whispered, "You know dear, if this was one of their episodes, one of the diners would fall dead from his chair at any moment, poisoned!"

Jane shuddered. "Oh, I hope not!"

Mitzi clapped her hands again. "Don't worry, it's only make-believe. Make-believe is such fun."

Jane nodded uncertainly. "I'm not sure I have a very good imagination."

Mitzi grew serious. "Jane, you must have confidence in your intellect. If you think your imagination is weak and your mind is dull, it is not that there is anything wrong with it, it's because it has never been used or stimulated. Like a muscle which is out of trim. There's no such thing as clever. Some people take more interest in their minds. That's all. Develop your mind and your body will follow!"

Jane brightened. She had never for a moment supposed she had hidden genius, but if it put as much fun into her life as it seemed to put into Mitzi's, it was worth a try. Jane was inquisitive to hear more about Lucian and

Diana. She took several sips of mineral water. Mitzi had been emphatic earlier.

"Always drink water with wine. The French do, and it is especially important in hot climates, though of course," with a chuckle, "in places like Egypt from bottles only, and then only the international brands."

Gently Jane drew her companion back from her reverie. "You hinted earlier that there was something mysterious about this envelope which I have not yet received."

Mitzi dabbed her lips with her napkin. They had both finished their main course. The waiter cleared the plates, and Mitzi asked for a pause before ordering dessert.

"It's rather strange and it goes back to the war. I do not know the exact details because Lucian never spoke in precise terms about it."

The story Mitzi went on to tell was as sinister as it was surprising. Had it not come from Mitzi, Jane would have found it hard to believe. According to Lucian, at the darkest hours of the war, when it seemed to many that Britain faced certain defeat, a group of top civil servants, senior members of the armed services, members of the intelligence services and certain politicians including one or two ministers, secretly conspired that they would supplant Churchill's "never surrender" regime and establish a government sympathetic to Germany with whom it would make peace. These traitors considered there was a higher duty to preserve the national fabric, even if subject to enemy rule, than allow the whole nation to be destroyed in a fight which could achieve no victory.

It seemed Lucian had been approached by the plotters, but although he allowed them to think he was sympathetic, and thus became aware of their plans, he never formally joined. Mitzi stressed that these people were not to be compared with Moseley and his Black Shirts, whose organisation was proscribed and whose leader interned. This group's leanings were absolutely covert. Thus it was, as the tide of war turned, they abandoned their plans, which remained forever undiscovered.

"Surely they were traitors!" observed Jane.

"Well, yes, they were *potential* traitors. Collaborators, perhaps, but unlike in France and the other conquered countries, they never had the opportunity to practise their treason," said Mitzi.

"But surely they would have been found out?"

"I don't think there was anything to find. It was all by word of mouth. They did not do anything to sabotage the war effort. Although I sometimes think that their support must at times have been half-hearted and this cannot have helped."

"Did the Germans know of this?"

"Well, of course, one does not know for sure. There are hints, as you know, that Hess was seeking to make contact with people who were sympathetic to Germany, but nothing came of it. He arrived too late for the group of which I am talking to break cover. Mind you, I think they conspired to make him appear a madman and I am not at all sure he was."

Jane found all this fascinating as a history lesson, but she could not quite see where it was leading.

"Did all this affect Lucian later?" she asked.

"Yes, that's the whole point. At the end of the war when it became clear that the things the Nazis had done were even more frightful than most people thought, Lucian was much troubled by the idea that although collaborators in the occupied countries were sought out and met with retribution, the potential collaborators in England got off without the smallest blemish to their reputations, because no one knew who they were."

Mitzi talked of this at some length. It seemed pretty clear that sections of MI5 knew mostly who the plotters were, but other sections which had been part of it, prevented any disclosure. Lucian had the feeling that there was a general hush-up by the establishment, so that those involved continued to serve in parliament and in the civil service and in government, as if nothing had happened, protected by the fact that in the strictest sense, nothing had.

As the years went by and Lucian's writing career developed, he resigned from the Home Office. He had become more and more disillusioned with both the top echelons of the civil service and their political masters. This attitude was the foundation of his penetrating interviewing skills when he became a broadcaster.

Jane wondered whether these issues had ever been discussed with her mother. She fancied not. She suspected that Lucian used his relationship with her mother to escape from the pressures and strains of his life rather than to engage her in them, but then again, what was this envelope about?

Mitzi leant close to Jane and spoke just above a whisper. "In the end he decided that the truth should be told. The way to do this was to include the facts in his own autobiography, including names. Some of these names were then still in public life, and even if this is no longer the case today, there will be sons who have replaced them. Some very big families were involved. Even," Mitzi's whisper was hardly audible even to Jane, "quite important Royalty! Mind you, nothing to do with the King and Queen. They were superb."

"But did he ever write this book?" whispered Jane.

"Well, this is the point. Everyone thought that his death intervened before he could write it. So did I, but later on I was not so sure."

"What made you unsure?"

"There was a rumour his publisher picked up from one or two of his inner circle, that he had finished the first draft before he died. And then," Mitzi hesitated at this point, "but then there was the death itself."

"What happened?"

"He was drowned at sea, fishing off the Cornish coast. He used to go down to one of the little coastal villages every year after the contact with your mother ceased. Fishing became his new passion. In 1967 a returning trawler found his boat bobbing around about four miles from the coast, empty. One of his three rods was missing, and it was assumed he had fallen overboard somehow, while trying to land a large fish. No body was found for weeks, which was awful. There was a memorial service and everything, but somehow I didn't feel it was final. Then eventually a torso with bits of limbs and some remnants of clothes including a fishing waistcoat, with all those pockets that they have, you know, for hooks and baits and things, was washed up. In a zip pocket was a little wallet containing his credit cards and so forth.

'I had the remains cremated in a completely private ceremony, except for the clergyman who took the service, he was a darling, and the police inspector, who was sweet as well. He gave me his huge white hankie to sob into, as my little lace one couldn't cope."

Even now, Jane could tell that Mitzi's eyes were moist. The waiter hovered with the sweet trolley. They each chose a slice of gateau, which turned out to be a lot lighter than it looked. In spite of the margarita and the wine, Jane was beginning to see things quite clearly. Although she did not drink much, she had a good head when she did. She must have inherited that from her mother.

"So you think the envelope contained information about the manuscript of the autobiography? Perhaps the place where it is hidden?"

"Exactly," nodded Mitzi.

This would not explain everything, but it would explain a certain amount. It would explain why someone was intent on rifling through papers. Had the burglar found anything? According to Mrs Tripper probably not. Whoever it was must be connected with the war-time plotters. Probably a member of an affected family, rather than a plotter, who would be too old and tottery for night time intrusions."

"The trouble is," said Jane through a mouthful of gateau, "it is difficult to know where to start looking. Mr Trubshaw almost certainly carried the information in his head, and now he is dead, we have no lead."

"Ah," said Mitzi, quaffing the last of her wine to wash down the cake, "we have three, not very strong, but leads nevertheless. The first is Lucian's publisher. He may know something. It's Bremmer House. Old Mr Bremmer has retired now, but his son is the chairman, and you should talk to him. Do not, under any circumstances, deal with underlings. They will know nothing. The second," went on Mitzi, "is the photo."

Jane had rather overlooked the snapshot. It had led her to Lucian and Mitzi. She had not thought it might take her further. She took it from her bag. Together she and Mitzi studied it. Up till now Jane had only taken an interest in the man standing beside her mother sitting in the doorway of what looked like a cottage. Although it was a black and white photograph, it was clear that the walls were covered in cream or white cement. The only distinguishing feature of the small section of the building shown in the snapshot was the huge pair of antlers fixed above the doorframe. Mitzi told Jane that she thought this was where the summer holidays had been spent.

"It looks like Scandinavia, Norway, or somewhere, but their cabins are usually of logs, not stone. And then, of course, he never took his passport with him. It was always sitting in the bureau when I went to get my own for my trips abroad. So it must be somewhere in England or Scotland." Mitzi was thoughtful. Then she went on. "You know, I began to think that the envelope contained the manuscript, but thinking about it now it couldn't have. I saw it once when the will was dealt with and on reflection it was too small." Her eyes now lit up. "But not too small to contain the deeds to a cottage."

"A cottage?"

"Yes, yes, dear! You see, it fits perfectly! Lucian and I were quite high earners, even in those days, and a cottage in the back of nowhere would have cost just a few hundred pounds. He was quite mean and liked remote places without hotels. He would begrudge renting so why not buy? Then leave it to your mother for her retirement."

"But why wait twenty years?"

Mitzi was not put off. "Well, maybe your father was still alive when he set up this extra bequest. He would have wanted Diana to receive it, well, when your father would not be troubled. Old-fashioned again, you know. Or maybe," Mitzi drew close and dropped her voice to a conspiratorial whisper, "maybe he made the bequest after he had written the manuscript. Maybe the cottage is where it is hidden!"

Jane was struggling. "But Mitzi, if the manuscript is there, why wait twenty years? Lucian would have known that Daddy was dead, which destroys your first theory. Your second theory makes no sense on its own!"

Mitzi pursed her lips and spread her hands before her on the table. Shortly she turned to Jane, who caught the expression in her eyes. It was quite penetrating.

"No dear. You are right. There is more to tell." She smiled a touch sheepishly. "It was silly of me to try and hold this back. About five years ago Harold Trubshaw came over to Cambridge to visit his old college. He did not do well, you know. A Third in History. Too much socialising. Anyway, we had dinner. Here as it happens. He drank a little too much, which was not unusual, then told me in strict confidence that Lucian had completed the manuscript before his death. He'd left it your mother, Diana, but after she died it was to come to you with some property. All this has been organised in such a way as to bypass the probate and so on, so as to be kept secret. That was why Harold, and not a lawyer, was involved. He would not say what property because I think he already felt he had said too much."

Jane was stunned. "Mitzi, why did you not tell me this at the beginning?"

Mitzi's face broke into another sheepish smile. "Unforgivable. Put it down to a lack of judgement. I felt you had so much to take on board. I thought I would try and spread it out somehow!"

Jane was not sure what to say, but Mitzi's composure returned. Her eyes twinkled. "You see, dear, I do so want to develop our friendship and I did not want you to be overwhelmed when I discovered you knew nothing."

Mitzi smiled again, this time with her usual confidence restored. Jane was reassured, even touched, but her mind stayed with the unravelling mystery.

"But why did Lucian not leave it all to you and, again, why wait the twenty years?"

"Well, he left me very comfortable with everything else. If the property was his love nest, sorry dear, you know what I mean, it would not be appropriate. With my German origins he probably thought that I was not the best person to handle the manuscript as I would lack credibility. Sour grapes and all that. People can still be quite anti-German over war issues. Harold told me that the twenty-year gap was to wait for a climate when there would be fewer around to try and block publication. The younger generation would be taking a more objective view of the war period. Mind you," Mitzi added after a momentary pause, "he was not expecting to die so early."

That made sense, certainly. But there was one more question. Jane sipped her wine before asking it. "Why did Lucian direct that whatever it actually is came to me?"

Mitzi laughed. "Oh that's easy! It's very Lucian. You were your mother's child. What was hers was yours!"

Mitzi was right. Jane was almost convinced. But how on earth could she locate the cottage?

"You mentioned a third clue?"

"He always took with him a pair of hobnailed boots."

"Hobnailed boots?"

"Yes, the sort they use for climbing and walking in the hills. Nowadays, I expect, they are made of synthetic rubber or something."

A cottage near mountains. That meant the Lake District, Wales or Scotland. It narrowed the area of search to many hundreds of square miles. Jane tried to persuade herself it was not hopeless.

"I shall start with Mr Bremmer."

Mitzi nodded.

Jane's heartbeat quickened. She knew who might be able to give advice, if it came to searching for cottages near mountains. She let her hand drop beside her chair and slipped the photo back into her handbag beside her feet. It was getting late and time to go.

"You said you were not driving?" asked Jane anxiously. She was not sure that either of them would pass breath tests.

"No, I never drive. The porter will call me a taxi. Normally I go everywhere by bike."

"Really?" Jane almost said "at your age", but stopped.

"It keeps me fit. It is the best way to travel in Peking," laughed Mitzi, "but also in Oxford or Cambridge."

The actors had finished their second bottle of wine and had started on brandies in enormous glasses. As the two women passed their table, Mitzi stopped.

"We're off to celebrate the fact we survived the meal." The two men regarded her, bemused, from beneath heavy lids. Mitzi chuckled mischievously. "You must forgive me, I'm a fan, and whenever you two go to dinner somewhere, somebody always falls off a chair, dead."

Realisation brought a moment's sobriety, a hearty laugh and autographs on a pad instantly produced by Mitzi from her handbag. Jane stood by in astonishment. As they reached the foyer, her companion explained.

"I love collecting autographs from entertainers. I often send off for them. They always respond as long as you enclose a self-addressed stamped envelope."

A taxi was called and Mitzi dropped Jane at her hotel. The lift was worth accepting. It was not that she feared an attack, but the effects of the cocktail and the wine were beginning to take hold.

As Jane made her way up to her room at the hotel she was buoyant. No doubt the wine helped, but she felt a sense of relief. She liked Mitzi enormously and the revelations about Lucian and her mother were really not too bad after all. The best part was that it ended when Diana met her father. Of course there was this business of the bequest. Probably a manuscript and a cottage, or more melodramatic, a manuscript *in* a cottage.

Jane was aware that she could turn her back on all of it. It was an unofficial bequest without any formal record. She could ignore what she did not have and return to her sheltered life. The cottage, if it existed, would fall down with neglect and the manuscript rot. This was a tempting course to set. Yet, having made such good progress? Then there was Tim Gulliver, alias Paul Harvey. Asking for his help to find this place or whatever would be such a good excuse for making contact. Then again, did she want to make contact? Her life had been so, well, so under control. *Her* control. Did she want the excitement, the turbulence even, of a personal relationship? Mind you, there was nothing to say anything would come of it. He might be married even. God forbid!

As Jane slipped the key into her door, she resolved to leave the whole issue on the back burner of her mind, for tonight at least. She could decide in the morning or in a day or two. There was no urgency. Better to take her time.

The room was cosy though quite small. Cramped for two people, thought Jane. She eyed the tea making facilities. Better not. It would keep her awake. Then she spotted a sachet of instant drinking chocolate. That would be perfect! Jane boiled the kettle.

Beside the bed there was a full-length mirror. Jane began to undress, taking an interest in her body, gradually revealed beneath peeling layers of silk and cotton. Naked, she sipped her freshly brewed nightcap and studied her own curving image. Sexy? What was sexy exactly? She touched her breasts. Her nipples came to life. If *he* saw her like this would he like it? Jane blushed at her own thoughts, startled at her wayward mind. She wondered about touching herself down there, that place she never went near except for hygiene. She began to caress her stomach but stopped short. This was getting silly! She had lost herself to wine for goodness sake! Perhaps another shower might be best. Jane drained her cup and stepped into the bathroom.

Later, feeling a little guilty at the sensations she had experienced under the cascading water, Jane reached a decision. She would search for the cottage.

CHAPTER SIX

Back home in Harvestdown, Jane's emotions were mixed. She disliked being away, so it was good to be in familiar surroundings. Yet in Cambridge she had caught an atmosphere of living which was new to her. The town itself, of course, had that beautiful, ageless quality of tranquillity and learning. Yet in the midst of what could well have been stuffiness, Mitzi was not at all stuffy. She found herself drawn to Mitzi's sense of fun and adventure. Jane felt her life had been enriched through her new acquaintance with this sparkling eccentric, in whose company and at whose expense she was shortly to go on the adventure of her life, to Egypt. The Pyramids. The Sphinx. The desert.

She had called on Mitzi again in the morning, following their dinner, before setting off on her journey for Sussex. By this time, all the arrangements had been completed. The travel agent had been contacted, and rooms and flights booked. They were to stay at Giza. "Cairo is fun to visit, but awful to stay in." The hotel chosen seemed to be of the luxury class. "Within its bounds we shall be cosseted with all the amenities of civilisation. Outside, things will be quite different. That's the fun!"

Mitzi clapped her hands again. Jane laughed. She did not often laugh. This time she laughed because she was happy.

Mitzi's mood changed as they were sipping coffee. "You know, Jane, when I told you about Lucian's death last night, there was something I missed out."

"Missed out?"

"Yes. I think he was murdered."

Jane thought of the newspaper cuttings. "There were rumours of foul play at the time of his death, weren't there?"

"Yes, dear, there were. Some years ago I visited the fishing village and talked to one or two of the fishermen. They insisted that the day Lucian set out on his fatal voyage, he had another man with him."

"The mysterious companion?"

"Yes."

"Do you know who that could have been?"

"No, and he was never heard of again."

"But why on earth should Lucian have been murdered?"

"I think it was to do with his autobiography. I think they wanted to stop him writing it."

"But you said last night that you thought he had already written it?"

"Yes, but I don't think they knew that at the time."

"Who is *they*?"

Mitzi shook her head. "One can never tell."

Jane was not yet frightened. Mystified and intrigued, certainly and perhaps just a little anxious, but she felt herself sharp and alert and ready to make decisions. The first of these was to make a visit to Lucian's publisher in London. She was less decisive about the scrap of paper with the phone number. She wanted to ring, but she was not sure that she should, and even if she did, she was not sure what to say. Well no. She knew exactly what to say, but she was not sure that it was right to say it. But the important thing was to find the cottage. Yes, she must find that.

Her difficulties ended two days after her return. There were two items in the post that morning. Her bank statement - goodness, that much! She must make some more investments. And an envelope from her agent containing another handwritten, sealed envelope within. She tore this open, with a quickening pulse, wondering what it could be. It was a short letter from Tim Gulliver on a piece of blue writing paper, but strangely without an address at the top. It said,

Dear Jane

I have to go to London on Friday the 23rd and will be at the Speaker's Arms just off Parliament Square near the Houses of Parliament, between 12.30 and 2.00. If you would care for a drink and a snack, please join me there. Maybe you could combine the visit with a shopping trip.

I hope this reaches you. I do not know your address, but I found out your agent from the publishers of The Nature Lover's Guides.

Regards,
Tim

What a perfect coincidence. She would go and see Mr Bremmer, the publisher, then meet Tim. She rang their office to make an appointment. A snooty secretary tried to put her off.

"Mr Bremmer is very busy. What is it concerning?"

"A missing autobiography."

The line went silent while the secretary consulted her boss. Moments later she was back on the line. "I'm afraid Mr Bremmer is too busy to see anyone for the next three weeks. He has suggested..."

With a flash of inspiration, Jane interrupted, "Tell him the autobiography is by Lucian Feyrbaeme."

Silence again. Then a man's voice, "Did you say you were coming to London on Friday?"

"Yes, I would be free at eleven."

"That would be fine," came the crisp reply.

Jane was a little apprehensive of her journey to London. She took the train. She found the crowds at Victoria daunting. So many tourists. How strange that London had become a tourist city. They came for its past, surely. Hub of an empire, upon which the sun never set. Yet now, upon which the sun had set forever. "And a good thing, too," thought Jane. She disliked imperialism.

She took one look at the teeming throng vanishing into a dark cavern over which was a sign saying *Underground* and turned away. She could not possibly cope with that. Which bus route would take her to Long Acre? Perhaps a taxi would be easiest. It turned out not to be far, but the price! Dear me, she must not do that again. The cabby, suave and in an immaculately pressed blue shirt and dark glasses, gave her a surly look. The tip had been rather mean, but at those sort of prices he would have to make do, Jane thought firmly. As she entered the foyer of *Bremmer House plc*, she suspected that behind the dark glasses he probably had quite nice eyes.

"Can I help you?" A bounce of hair and the flash of a humourless grin drew Jane towards the receptionist.

"Mr Giles Bremmer is expecting me."

"Have you an appointment?"

"Yes, at eleven o'clock."

"And your name?"

"Jane Block."

A quick phone call, then the receptionist flashed the smile of confidence again. "His secretary will be down to collect you shortly."

Jane perched on the edge of a leather sofa. She clutched her bag on her knees. The lift doors parted. A woman so formidable that Jane almost took to flight, approached. Afterwards, Jane could recollect little of her appearance, except an impression of frameless glasses, blue-rinsed hair and an enormous bosom.

"Miss Block?" Jane nodded. "Please come with me. Mr Bremmer is rather busy. He was, however, able to squeeze you in, but we must not keep him waiting."

Jane shook her head, then nodded, searching desperately for her voice. As they rose in the lift, she decided against any attempt at camaraderie with this battleaxe. She needed to conserve her scattering confidence for the meeting with Mr Giles Bremmer.

His office was large, but cosy. It gave the impression of being established in its present form for many years, and she guessed it had previously been used by his father. Many times, perhaps, Lucian would have crossed this threshold. The desk, the various chairs and the conference table were in the style of Chippendale, although Jane, her artistic talent making her observant of small detail, thought she identified them as high quality Edwardian copies. Maples, probably.

Giles Bremmer was charming. Why should such a man employ such a terrifying secretary? Perhaps he was too nice and needed protection. He held out his hand.

"This is a wonderful surprise. My father always looked forward to Lucian Feyrbaeme's autobiography, but the author's death intervened. Would you like some coffee?" Giles indicated a chair at right angles to his desk.

Jane declined the coffee. She feared that manoeuvring a cup would reveal a shaking hand. Giles continued talking.

"I met him just a few times, as my father, Cedric Bremmer, looked after him. Cedric was the second generation. My grandfather, Sergei, founded the business when he arrived penniless from Russia in the 1880's."

This was all very interesting, thought Jane, but how to begin? She was not being given an opportunity.

"Are you an agent?"

"No, I'm an artist."

"How interesting."

"Well, an illustrator for books."

"For books?"

"*The Nature Lover's Guides.*"

"Oh, very high quality work. How are you connected with this autobiography?"

"It's a rather peculiar situation," began Jane.

Giles became attentive. Jane gave a brief outline of her inheritance and the note she had received from Harold Trubshaw, of whose tragic death Giles was already aware. She explained that as a result of a conversation with Mitzi, she thought of the possibility that a first draft of the autobiography existed and wondered if the publisher had information.

"Ah, dear me, no. I was rather hoping that *you* would have information. It's a manuscript we would very much like to acquire, but like you, we are uncertain whether it was ever written. I had thought from the phone message," his voice took a slight edge, "that you had positive information."

They talked further, but of no substance. Jane saw Giles glance sideways towards the clock. He began to excuse himself.

"I'm sorry to rush you. I have a meeting followed by a luncheon appointment, but I was keen to meet you." As he walked her to the door, he took her arm. "I know you will not want to talk business now, but should you find the manuscript, please be assured that we would be very interested to acquire the publishing rights. We would be prepared to offer a very substantial advance. Six figures." Then, "At least," he added after a pause.

Jane blinked. The battleaxe appeared. Jane nodded her good-byes. In the street she recovered her wits, realising that she was caught at the centre of an unfolding drama involving not only reputations, but money in very large sums. *At least* six figures! That meant, with a push, to seven! Jane's mouth went dry. If she could find this manuscript, she would not have to worry about taxi fares. It was not too far to Parliament Square and the walk would do her good. She was a little apprehensive of her next appointment of the day.

Should she keep the rendezvous at all? Was it not a little cheap to accept an invitation from a stranger, to meet in a pub? Yet, how else was she to meet strangers who might later become friends? She needed friends. And she needed to find that cottage. Seven figures! It was surprising that people were still so interested in Lucian's manuscript. Even if he did name names, it was history. Interesting history, certainly, but surely not worth seven figures. Her generation, after all, hardly cared. It was too long ago. How many were still alive who had taken part? Not all that many. Not enough to make the book worth a fortune. But publishing was a strange business.

High above her head the sign swung back and forth in the wind. The Speaker's Arms. Jane had walked down Whitehall and across Parliament Square. She had not really been this way since her teens. Things had not changed that much. But the crowds! Everywhere there were people standing with camcorders and cameras. Opposite Big Ben, the buildings surrounding the underground station looked seedy and unkempt. Stalls and souvenir shops selling rubbish. Echoes, she suspected, of Cairo without the hot weather. Perhaps she had the right idea, after all, to escape from all this.

The bar was crowded and smoky. People jostled for drinks. What an odd place to meet. She could see no sign of him. Then she noticed the stairs to the restaurant. That must be it. On the first floor things were quieter and better ordered. It was more of a bar with tables than a full-blown restaurant, but bright, competent girls were there to organise the seating and take the orders. She looked around. There was no sign of Tim. Her heart sank in disappointment. Then she looked at her watch. Twelve fifteen. Oh dear, she had not realised.

"A table?"

"Yes please. For two."

Would she like a drink while she waited?

"A glass of white wine."

Supposing he did not turn up? Maybe he was here already, in that crush downstairs. He would look up here. He was that type. She could tell.

She was refreshed by a few sips of wine. She rummaged for her compact and put on some lipstick. She would wait until twenty to one, then order, eat her meal, enjoy it and go. She could always ring, after all, because she had the number.

Her heart missed a beat. There he stood in the doorway. Taller than she remembered, certainly well over six foot. He was immaculately turned out in a dark grey suit, cut to fit his frame perfectly, and with an absence of concessions to fashion which told of the best of tailors, probably Saville Row. A red rose sat in the buttonhole of his jacket. From this buttonhole, too, hung a thin gold chain which disappeared into his breast pocket. The brown eyes twinkled at once and smiled in recognition. Jane smiled back. She felt herself radiating happiness and relief. They shook hands. A little formal perhaps.

"I was early," she said.

"You were punctual," he replied.

The girl approached. Jane decided to be bold.

"The first drink is on me."

Tim beamed and enquired what she was drinking, then ordered the same. The menu was rather limited, but it did not matter.

Their conversation was animated. Jane was glad of her meeting with Mitzi, because it had provided a sort of rehearsal and sharpened her mind. They spoke of many things. Her painting, his writing, mountains. As Jane became more confident, she told Tim a little of her story. She kept the manuscript and the wartime traitors to herself, but she told him of the photograph. She had it with her. He looked carefully.

"Probably Scotland," he said at length. "It could be a croft, although the antlers are unusual."

Jane almost asked him for his help there and then, but she felt it better to wait until another meeting. She thought he might offer, she sensed he wanted to, but perhaps he felt it best to wait.

Towards the end of the meal, a man entered the restaurant, not as tall as Tim, younger and not so good-looking. He had blond hair and his blue eyes were piercing and humourless. Tim looked up and for a second Jane detected the jolt of recognition freeze momentarily in his eyes.

Jane leant forward and whispered, "Do you know that person?"

Tim looked at her. There was a second's hesitation. "No. I thought I did, but he is not the person I had in mind."

"Ah," said Jane. She thought he was being untruthful. Not lying. Just an untruth. There was all the difference.

Soon Tim called for the bill, explaining that he had to keep an appointment. She offered her share but was waved aside. He paid in cash, which surprised her. Nowadays business people used credit cards. Mind you, he was an author.

Tim looked at Jane. "You have my telephone number. This time you must promise to ring. If not, I shall insist that you give me your address."

"I promise I'll ring."

"Soon?"

"Soon."

He took the rose from his buttonhole. "This is your token."

In a moment he was gone. Jane clutched the rose and felt happy. The encounter had been a complete success. She had even asked him why he was so reclusive as an author. He explained he worked as a consultant with a public relations company seconded to a government department and he did not want a public persona to clash with his business profile. This made so much sense. Jane wondered why she had not worked it out herself.

With her confidence growing, Jane decided that she liked him. Yes, she liked him a lot. From the corner of the restaurant she felt the cold blue eyes staring at her. Quickly, she gathered her belongings and made her way back to Victoria. As she settled in the train, she relived her date. Yes, it was a date. Dare she admit it, her first. She understood now why he had chosen that pub, situated as it was right at the heart of the government structure. There were a few tourists there, but she suspected that the rest were civil servants, maybe even some MP's. She had the feeling that Tim knew the place well and was known in turn. His working local, so to speak. Jane reminded herself that she was engaged in a search for a manuscript which may contain details of treason. What an extraordinary turn her life had taken. No wonder Harold Trubshaw had called it a burden! But as the vision of Tim's handsome face erased the suburban tedium of south-west London clattering past, Jane was not at all sure that it was.

CHAPTER SEVEN

At home, Jane found herself unsure of her next move. Her life had taken on so many new dimensions that she was afraid she was losing control of it. She took refuge, as she had done before when times were difficult, in cooking. She made expeditions to local farm shops to buy fresh provisions and produce. She baked bread, pastry and a fruitcake that was large enough to last her for months. She roasted a piece of gammon to provide cold ham in case of need, so much better than buying slices in the shops, and made a large casserole which contained quite a bit of red wine. With her cupboards, tins and fridge well stocked, she felt much more relaxed, in control of her life and able to make decisions again.

At length she made up her mind that she would begin her search for the cottage when she returned from the trip to Egypt with Mitzi. She would ring Tim and let him know she was going away, and promise to make further contact on her return. She could use the excuse of ringing to thank him for lunch. His knowledge of hills and mountains would prove essential in her quest. She must go about it the right way to be sure to persuade him to help. Mind you, she would have to be careful. It would not do to give him the wrong ideas.

She had arranged to contact Mitzi again, so that they could finalise their plans, or rather, she could hear Mitzi's plans for the trip. A thought suddenly struck Jane. Now she had such an ample supply of food, it would be a good idea to ask Mitzi to stay. So she rang and it was all arranged. The day after tomorrow. Jane was not sure that Mitzi would want to make the journey by train, but this turned out to be no problem at all.

"I shall love it, dear. I have a senior citizen's railcard, so I travel for practically nothing."

It would mean arriving at Liverpool Street Station and crossing over to Victoria. She would meet Mitzi at Arundel. There was a squeal of delight down the line.

"Arundel Castle, what fun! Seat of the Earl Marshall of England. That's a perfect place to travel to."

"The Earl Marshall of England?"

"Yes, dear, the Duke of Norfolk."

"Oh." Jane was vague about these things and moved on to luggage. "Are you sure you will be able to manage with your bag? There might be quite a long walk from the train to the taxis."

"That'll be no trouble. I shall find a porter."

"A porter! I'm not sure that these days you will find one."

"Nonsense, dear. I always find porters, and if there aren't any, I shall use one of the male passengers."

So it was all settled. Within a few minutes of the phone call, Jane had made up the bed in the spare room and since all her other preparations were complete, she had an idea how to use the day in between to keep herself busy. She would ring Celia, and if she were free, drive over to Newbury tomorrow to tell her of her coming trip and see if she could borrow any suitable clothes for hot climates. Jane was not keen to buy anything, because she might never use the things again and it would be a waste of money.

Yes, Celia would be in and she would be thrilled. "Cairo! How wonderful! I have the very things you need."

This time it was lunch, which was much better than the evening because Jane must not be late with a guest the next day, and the return journey would be in daylight. Better than last time, in that awful storm. Jane shuddered when she remembered her nightmare afterwards.

She enjoyed her visit more than before. Celia was less gushing, and the intuition of their old friendship seemed to have been re-established. Celia took Jane up to her bedroom, which was enormous, and through to her dressing room which was as big as a double bedroom in most houses. Jane had never seen so many clothes. Fortunately, although the two women were a rather different shape, they were more or less the same size, and Jane ended up borrowing a smart linen jacket, a casual straw hat with a big brim, and a thin silk dress for the evenings.

While Jane was going through the process of trying things on, Celia left to receive a phone call. Jane saw that there was another door from the dressing room leading to a bathroom. This was very up to date, including two marble washbasins side by side, on a his and hers basis. At the far end of the bathroom was another door, which Jane found opened into Monty's dressing room. It contained an almost identical range of built-in cupboards and drawers as Celia's dressing room, together with a mahogany shelf surrounded by mirrors, on which sat hair brushes, combs and other oddments. What luxury, thought Jane, but what a lot of room a man takes up! She had not thought of that.

After lunch, Celia took Jane into the drawing room. She had not been in here before. It was sumptuous and formal. A mixture of silks, brocade and porcelain ornaments blended with pieces of French Empire. The centrepiece was a grand piano, covered with family photographs in silver frames. The biggest was Celia's latest wedding photograph.

"So this is Monty?" said Jane with interest.

"Yes, he's such a poppit."

Jane studied the images. "Where is Monty now?"

"Oh, he got back from New York, but he's flown off again to Rio. Foreign Office business again."

"Is Brazil where he has his estates?"

"No, that's Argentina. They are not his estates, they're his mother's, but he benefits from a family trust. His father is English, he was an MP until the last election. She is the foreigner."

Father an MP. Son in the Foreign Office. Jane thought for a moment. She did not wish to seem rude, but she wanted to know.

"What does he do in the Foreign Office?"

"Do? Darling, what do any of them do!" Celia took Jane's arm. "One must never have any idea what one's husband does for a living, otherwise they will start telling you their problems. Once they bring their problems home, that's the end. The absolute end."

"Oh," said Jane uncertainly. Then brightly so as to seem conversational rather than inquisitive, "He sounds wonderful. How did you meet?"

Celia threw back her head and laughed. "At last you are taking an interest in men! And so you should. Your life would be transformed!" She put her arm round Jane's shoulders and gave her an affectionate hug.

"Monty met me at Pickards. At the fifteen year reunion. You did not come. Your mother had just died, I think. Anyway, it was not your scene. Monty was with his sister. You remember Victoria Flemington?"

Good Heavens! Jane, though she knew Celia's married name, had not made the connection.

Now she exclaimed, "That Flemington! Victoria your sister-in-law?", adding before she could stop herself, "God, how awful!"

Celia brushed it aside. "Don't worry, darling. She married her own millions to impoverished nobility in Leicestershire. Now Lady Pulverton, she is blissfully happy and ignores us"

They spent a happy afternoon, and Jane left just after four, arriving back home in good time for an early supper. She was not really hungry, but she decided to try a slice or two of her newly cooked ham, just to make sure that it had turned out the way she wanted.

As she lay in bed that night, her mind turned over a curious discovery. Celia's Monty was not in Rio for she had seen him yesterday in London. The man with the thinning blond hair and the cold blue eyes in the Speaker's Arms was the same man who stood arm in arm with his bride in

Celia's wedding photograph on the grand piano in her sumptuous drawing room. Pure chance probably. Cheating on Celia no doubt. He was that type, you could tell. Victoria's brother! That awful girl was a cross between a prig, a bully, a cheat and a nymphomaniac in the making.

Nevertheless curious photographs were beginning to loom larger than they ought in Jane's hitherto predictable life. Jane was uncertain how she should feel, but clearly it was growing less predictable by the day.

Odd really. She was feeling quite good about it.

CHAPTER EIGHT

Next day, Mitzi was one of only two passengers to alight from the train at Arundel Station shortly after midday. The other was a morose looking teenager with long hair, whom Jane mistakenly mistook for a girl, but she felt sad for him. He was morose because like so many others, he could see little in his future to put a spring into his step or a light in his eye. Soon he would rely on the stimulus of alcohol or worse. Maybe he would work, maybe not. Who could tell? Certainly not the Government ministers, shuffling out their jobs between them. Nor the yelling mass on the opposite benches who wanted to replace them.

Mitzi was waving from the end of the platform. She appeared to have got out of the first carriage. It seemed miles when Jane finally reached her.

"I was afraid the platform would be short, dear, at a country station, so I got in at the front."

"Wise precaution," puffed Jane as they embraced.

Jane took the suitcase. This turned out to be a splendid artifact of stout leather and rectangular shape with many sticky labels, recording travel to exotic places. It was exactly like a piece of luggage that one would see in a film. The difference, thought Jane, as she struggled to lift it from the ground, was that luggage in films was always as light as a feather and carried by actors and actresses without a thought. The modern sort with wheels would be much better for an old lady. What could she have in here? It was only two nights after all. At last they reached the car park. Jane opened the rear door and put the case between the seats. The car sank on its springs. Mitzi settled herself beside Jane, beaming.

"Both trains were punctual. I'm always lucky with travel," she continued. "Very rarely a hold-up. You were right, dear, about the porters, but I saw this nice young man. He took me all the way to the taxi rank carrying the suitcase. It was only when we got there that I discovered he was on the platform to get *on* the train, not get off it. So he had to go all the way back. So good of him!"

Jane smiled to herself.

Back at The Hollies, Mitzi took a keen interest in everything. Jane was worried that she might find the spare room rather small, and even thought of giving Mitzi her own room.

"This is just perfect," exclaimed Mitzi. "I like small rooms. They remind me of being on board ship and when one is away, one only has a few oddments, so one doesn't need space."

Jane remembered the weight of the suitcase, now on the bed, and was not sure. Mitzi went to the window.

"What a perfect view! The Downs are lovely. That's one of the snags of the country around Cambridge, so flat. I love the hills. They watch over you and keep you safe."

It was later after supper, Mitzi claimed never to have been so well-fed in her life, following a busy afternoon which included a tour of the village and a walk quite some distance up the footpath towards the hills, when Mitzi said, "Are you any nearer finding the cottage?"

Jane was able to say only that she thought Scotland was the most likely location. Mitzi asked to see the photo. Jane fetched it from her handbag. Mitzi looked at it.

"Have you a magnifying glass, dear?"

"Upstairs in the studio."

Together they went up to the workroom. Mitzi sat at the table that Jane used when she was not at her easel and turned on the spotlight. She looked through the powerful glass Jane had handed to her. Mitzi pointed at the box containing the pot plants.

"There is lettering here. You can just make it out."

She handed the photo and the glass to Jane who looked at the letters. Jane gradually made out the letters *PORTREE*.

"That's a place," said Mitzi, "in Scotland somewhere, I forget where."

"Wait, I have an atlas," said Jane excitedly.

She pulled a survivor from her schooldays from a shelf and looked through the index. Yes, there it was. She turned to the page and followed the reference.

"It's on the Isle of Skye. I think it's the largest town."

"Yes, of course," said Mitzi, "I knew I'd heard of it. There are mountains on the Isle of Skye. It's quite an important range called the Cuillins. Famous climbers go there to train." She had another look at the photo with the glass. "This is an old fish box. There must have been a lot of fishing off Skye in those days. The evidence all points to Skye! I think you now have your location!"

Jane agreed that this would make good sense. She had never been to Scotland, let alone the Isle of Skye, but it looked a small island, so perhaps in the end the search would not prove as fruitless as she feared. At least when she got back from Egypt she would know where to begin.

The rest of Mitzi's visit was a great success. Jane's own existence caught the pulse of Mitzi's energy. They finalized their plans for the trip which was

A Gift of Treason

now only ten days away. More accurately put, Mitzi explained her plans to Jane. They were to fly to Cairo by the Egyptian airline, it seemed. Jane was apprehensive at this.

"It's always better," explained Mitzi, "when flying to places like that to use the national airline. We will be much better looked after on arrival. You must pay the compliment of showing confidence in their facilities and institutions."

They were not to stay in Cairo, but at Giza. This was right beside the great Pyramids, and healthier. As promised, the hotel was in the international luxury class, a former palace of the deposed King Farouk, with enormous grounds providing every comfort, facility and amenity. Jane was bewildered by the scale. Nothing before in her life had exceeded two stars.

Mitzi explained. "As we are only there for six days, we shall not have time to acclimatize. So we will use the hotel for all meals and for leisure. We can explore by taxi and by foot. This way we stand a better chance of avoiding the inevitable tummy upsets."

Jane nodded enthusiastically. She remembered Spain.

"And always travel light, dear. Make do with the minimum of things. We do not have to put on a show when it's just the two of us together. You need a light, strong bag designed for air travel. I wouldn't dream of taking Bertram."

"Bertram?"

"Yes dear, my leather suitcase. I always call it Bertram, after the dear old professor who gave it to me forty years ago."

"Oh yes, I see."

When finally Jane put Mitzi and Bertram back on the train for the return journey and waved goodbye, she was quite worn out. Keeping up with this old lady was proving quite a strain on her metabolism. She looked forward to the trip with apprehension. On her return to England her search on the Isle of Skye for the cottage for the snapshot would seem like a rest by comparison. Jane figured she would probably need it.

The next ten days passed quickly, as she made her preparations, completed outstanding commissions for illustrations well before their deadline, and saw to the other small, but important, details of travel like currency and inoculations. As she busied herself about the village, tramped the footpaths or worked in her brightly-lit studio, she felt herself becoming sharper, more aware. Almost as if after some long hibernation she were coming alive.

Yes, that was it.
Coming alive!

CHAPTER NINE

It was Jane's firm belief, when she finally returned to The Hollies from Cairo, that she would remember every detail of the trip for the rest of her life. She would be eternally grateful to Mitzi, not just for taking her, but for showing her how to extract value from every passing moment.

They had arranged to meet at the airport by the check-in desk. Jane arrived, nervously complete, with her new suitcase, purchased not too expensively from a department store, clutching a shoulder bag with the essential documents and effects for the journey and feeling a little self-conscious in the straw hat and linen jacket lent to her by Celia. She saw Mitzi instantly. She was wearing a cream cotton safari suit, by no means new, but clearly from the best vintage, and a battered but quite splendid straw hat with a huge brim. She was waving a parasol to attract Jane's attention. Her luggage consisted of one quite modern suitcase and a canvas bag in the shape of a small sack with shoulder straps and an enormous sunflower embroidered on the side.

They greeted each other with a warm embrace before going through the process of checking tickets and weighing in the cases. Mitzi refused to give up her parasol.

"This is hand luggage. On no account will I surrender it!" The clerk demurred.

She confided in Jane. "I had one years ago, but it fell to pieces. I found this at a car boot sale. Cost a pound. I don't think they knew what it was and confused it with an umbrella. It's beautifully made, 1920's I should think."

She pushed it up with a flourish for all to see. Nearby passengers were sent reeling back, a business executive of florid appearance having come within a fraction of losing an eye.

The journey was smooth and comfortable, although as always in tourist class, cramped. Fortunately the plane was not too crowded, so they could spread themselves a little. Jane's nervousness soon wore off, helped by another of Mitzi's aperitifs with what she called *zing*.

"I don't think we can ask for margaritas, not back here in the steerage, so we'll make our own vodka martinis. Vodka is less enervating than gin, especially when flying."

Bemused, Jane agreed. Beneath her breath she muttered, "How pre-war," which provoked a little giggle that Mitzi did not notice.

Because it was an afternoon flight and changing time zones, they arrived in Cairo at one o'clock in the morning. Jane was stunned when the pilot announced over the intercom that the outside temperature was thirty-four degrees centigrade.

"In the middle of the night?" She looked at Mitzi in alarm.

"Don't worry, dear, the air is very dry, so you don't notice it. Anyway, the hotel is fully air-conditioned."

Baggage handling and the journey to the hotel were without incident. There was a small air-conditioned executive coach to meet them and one or two other passengers. The hotel was luxurious and of an architectural design which Jane had heard described in Spain as Moorish. Jane had been astonished to find that Mitzi spoke Egyptian with some fluency. The effect on the hotel staff was impressive. Quickly Mitzi had porters and receptionists running hither and thither. Soon the manager appeared resplendent in morning dress to escort them personally to their rooms.

Lack of sleep and the unfamiliar environment gave Jane a sense of unreality, as if she were acting a part. Nevertheless, for the very first time in her life she felt herself to be somebody of importance, which lifted her feeble self-esteem considerably. Breakfast was arranged for 10 am.

"We won't sleep after that, dear, and we can always have a siesta in the hot part of the day."

Before Jane dozed off, she remembered something that made her blush furiously in the darkness. She had attended her local surgery for inoculations. Mitzi had advised her to take every precaution, whether officially recommended or not. Old Dr Bakewell had given her the injections. As she had known him since she was a child, she felt safe with him, yet when it came to asking, her courage almost failed her.

"Is there anything else you need for this journey?" he murmured, writing up her notes.

"I would like to go on the pill," blurted out Jane.

Dr Bakewell looked up. "Have you been on it before?" he asked.

She knew he knew the answer was no. She shook her head.

"Have you met someone?"

She nodded.

"Have you had relations yet?" Dr Bakewell's terminology was rather old-fashioned.

Jane shook her head again. She took the prescription he handed her.

"I'm so pleased for you," said the doctor and gave her arm a squeeze as he walked her to the door. He went on, "It is my duty these days to just mention the usual health warnings to you."

Jane nodded again. As she stepped into the fresh air it felt as if her cheeks were on fire. She drove off with a lurch and a crash of gears. Dr Bakewell watched over the rim of his glasses from the window and smiled to himself. Up the road, Jane pulled over and stopped. She buried her head in her hands and sobbed. Sobbed with shame at being such a fool. In an age where women were as liberated as men, the climb out of her self-constructed Victorian cocoon was humiliating.

On this first morning at Giza Jane drew her curtains and looked directly at the Great Pyramid towering nearby. She felt a surge of emotion, a sort of welcome to the world outside the narrow confines of her own. The following days passed for her timelessly, as if caught up in an adventure which broke connection with all other events and measures. They visited the Pyramids, both during the day and again in the early dusk, so as to look down on the floodlit sphinx. Jane felt the ghosts of the Pharaohs at her elbow, a sense of knowledge and spiritual wisdom far exceeding the coarse science of the modern day.

They made two visits to Cairo. Once to the museum containing the antiquities, including the treasures of Tutankhamun's tomb. Mitzi knew every detail and turned out to be an informative and clever guide. The second was a visit to the bazaar, a sort of Cairo equivalent to Soho, where shopkeepers and traders operated much as they had done for centuries, but of course, with a significant eye to tourism.

On the journeys between Giza and Cairo, Jane could scarcely believe the driving. Mitzi had warned that such controls as traffic lights were treated as decorations. The drivers wove an intricate pattern in and out of the traffic at high speed without regard to lane discipline or road safety. Piles of wreckage at the side of the main highway, left from previous accidents, like hulks of armour in Sinai, bore witness to the risks. It was very different to progress in the 2CV, but nevertheless, Jane found it rather exhilarating. Mitzi sensed this, and smiling, patted Jane's knee.

"Have confidence in the people into whose hands you have committed your life and everything is more enjoyable."

At meals, which they always took at one of the hotel restaurants, there was ample time to get to know each other. Mitzi detected Jane's lack of self-confidence and worked gently to help her. They talked of Lucian and the manuscript.

"Why did Lucian decide to name names?" asked Jane.

"Lucian decided that history should know what had happened and who these people were. His closeness to me and knowledge of all that my parents had been through may have spurred him on."

"What happened to your parents, Mitzi?"

"They went to America. My father worked on the Manhatten Project with Oppenheimer."

"The Manhattan Project?"

"The atom bomb."

Jane was shocked. "How awful!"

"I agree, dear, but at the time he didn't see it as awful. He paid the price and died of cancer in 1952."

"I'm sorry."

"My mother could not reconcile herself to the fact that their flight from their homeland and their opposition to the Nazi terror had led them to play a part in creating a means of mass slaughter. She died first. She threw herself in front of a train when she learned my father had cancer."

Jane was distressed. She wished she had never asked. She put her hand on Mitzi's. "Mitzi, I'm so sorry, I didn't mean to pry. That is so sad."

"I coped at the time because I had Lucian and he was marvelous. Now, they would have been dead anyway, so it makes no difference."

There was a sinister incident on the trip. Jane was still confused by its meaning. They were in the bazaar. Because Mitzi spoke Egyptian and had been there before, they wandered somewhat from the tourist track. Soon they were lost. The streets grew narrower and dark. Jane peered through open doorways to see rooms full of old men, sucking at their hubble-bubbles. She grew frightened. Mitzi, too, grew anxious. She asked for directions. People seemed not to understand and turned their backs. Perhaps her dialect was wrong, or the accent foreign.

Suddenly Mitzi exclaimed, "Oh look, a European!"

At the end of an alley stood a man in a Panama hat and a white linen suit. He began to walk, and they followed him at a distance. He turned this way and that. They kept him in sight. At last they were back in the main thoroughfare and he disappeared into the crowd.

"How fortunate. I think he must have guessed we were lost, but was too much of a gentleman to impose himself," said Mitzi with relief.

Jane was not too sure. He had kept his distance, but at one point Jane was near enough to think she may have recognised the man from the Speaker's Arms, whom she now knew to be Celia's husband, Monty. Jane was shaken but said nothing. She could think of no reason why he should follow her to Egypt, except for the manuscript. He cannot have wished her any harm, because it would have been easy to abandon them to be murdered in the back alleys of the bazaar without anyone being the wiser. Later in the less threatening environment of the hotel, Jane felt she had been mistaken. She hoped so, anyway.

One morning, Jane rose earlier than Mitzi, so she decided to use the extra time she had gained in the day to walk up the slope from the hotel to the Pyramids. The sun was not yet high in the sky, but it was already hot. A drying wind blew from the south. Again Jane stood in awe, tiny, beneath the colossal structures. She from the space age, an age still ignorant of the meaning of this unprecedented feat of engineering from ages past. She stood and stared. Stone. Sun. Sand. Secrets. Jane lingered whilst currents of warm air caressed her bare skin, finding their way through the folds of her thin clothes. She wished that soon some of her own secrets would be secrets to her no longer.

Parting with Mitzi at the end of the adventure proved unexpectedly sad. In spite of the age gap, they were now genuine companions. Jane was enriched by the new experiences brought to her by Mitzi, who in turn was enlivened by the pleasure of freeing the younger woman from the constraints of her narrow lifestyle. Already there were plans for another journey. In the autumn, to Venice.

"Never been to Venice? My dear, we shall move it to the top of the list. An absolute priority. Life, without the Venice experience, is life impaired. Late September will be perfect. Not quite so overcrowded, nor too hot. Bring comfortable shoes. I will walk you off your feet!"

Jane was thrilled. Two expeditions in a year. She had never imagined anything like it would happen once in her life. Now twice in one year, with more to follow!

In Harvestdown there were other matters which pressed upon her with new urgency. The search for the cottage must now take priority. But there was something else, or rather, someone else. She had rung Tim Gulliver before setting off to Egypt, but he was out. Jane caught her breath as she heard his voice, somewhat crackly, telling her from an answering machine to leave her name and number. In fright, Jane slammed down the phone. She hated those things. They made her self-conscious, convinced she sounded stupid. But on the other hand, if she did not contact him until her return, he might abandon all hope. Jane rehearsed carefully what she was going to say and then rang again. Briefly she explained that she was going abroad for one week and would call again on her return. She considered leaving her number, but decided against it.

Soon she must call again. Was he really interested in her, or was he just being polite? Jane looked at herself in the mirror. Surely a man so handsome would have better opportunities. She did not even know yet if he was married. He seemed too relaxed for a married man, so she was fairly sure that if there had been a marriage, it was not current. Egypt had given her a tan which she thought had improved her looks, and gave her glamour potential which she had not previously considered. Maybe now was the time to try something new.

She had never given much thought to her appearance, but in a moment of daring she consulted yellow pages for a list of beauticians. She chose one in Chichester, and before her courage evaporated, dialled hastily to make an appointment that very afternoon. When she arrived, she hesitated at the door, but the manageress was charming, as well as young and pretty and seemed well capable of dealing with nervous customers. Indeed, she was positively excited by the arrival of the new client.

"You have a lovely face. Such well-defined features, and your hair is so soft. Within two hours we will make you irresistible!"

Jane blushed. How could they know why she was doing this?

Finally it was done. Jane paid the bill, beauty did not come cheap, and stepped into the sunshine of the precinct outside. She thought heads turned. Had they made her a freak? She looked nervously for her reflection, stealing a glance in a shop window. At last she began to accept what she should have known all along. She was possessed of a modest but striking beauty which most women would have spent years developing and exploiting. Instead, she had hidden it in the privacy of her little house, cut off from the passing world, stimulated only by such mundane distractions as rambles on the Downs and shopping for organic produce.

Back home, she now confidently dialled Tim's number. Again the recorded voice, but this time Jane was decisive. Would he ring as soon as possible? She left her number before replacing the phone on its rest.

A tingle of excitement ran up her spine.

CHAPTER TEN

Jane had to wait less than an hour for Tim to return her call. In the meanwhile, she had been sitting at her kitchen table sipping coffee and trying to make sense out of the conflicting events which had started to permeate her life following the arrival of the photo.

The most perplexing part was Monty. Why had he been in the pub that day? Had he been in Cairo? What did he do at the Foreign Office? Why did he lie to Celia as to his whereabouts? Was he in the Secret Service?

Jane was aware that some part of the security services reported to the Foreign Secretary, and she thought this was the overseas branch, which might explain Monty's appearance in Cairo, if, indeed, he was there at all. Nevertheless it seemed far too melodramatic to suppose that the security services could have an interest in her. It was no business of theirs anyway. It was a free country, and whatever was in the manuscript should be published and read by everyone. Well, probably not everyone, but anyone who was interested in that sort of thing. Were people interested, so long after the war? It was history after all. Would people really care? Probably not, but the media would care and they would whip up interest until eventually passions were raised over issues not previously thought about.

Jane reflected on how all this had disrupted her life, yet it was not all bad news. Meeting Mitzi had been an enriching experience, and Tim, well, if she had not gone to Winchester that day and chanced into that pub, she would never have met him. She could not be sure that the meeting would lead anywhere, but for the very first time in her life, she desperately wanted this relationship to develop.

Jane let the phone ring twice.
"Harvestdown 21165?"
"It's Tim. Sorry I was out when you rang."
Jane's heart skipped a beat. She put her invitation, casually, of course. Now that she was back from Egypt, wouldn't it be nice to meet? She was working on the project to find the cottage. He seemed to know a lot about Scotland, so it would be nice to talk about that, too. More relaxed at home than a pub. Why not Sunday lunch? This was a clever test. If he had a wife and family, he would hesitate about Sunday lunch.

"Yes, I'd love that. Sunday lunch would be a big treat. I'm a lousy cook."

"This Sunday, or are you busy?"

It would do fine. He would arrive about twelve thirty. Jane gave directions. So there was no wife.

Jane looked in her wardrobe and found the contents dowdy and old-fashioned. She set out in the 2CV to Portsmouth. There would be a good choice of fashion stores and boutiques, and as it was some distance, there would be little chance of her being recognised. Later, exhilarated by her purchases, she struggled with her burden of carriers and parcels back to the little car. When they were safely stowed, she locked the doors again, because there was something more she wanted to do. It would be tricky, but now she felt she had enough confidence to cope.

The bookshop was large and at first confusing. She found what she wanted under Health. To make the acquisition seem more everyday, she bought a cooking encyclopedia and a book on herbs. At the paydesk she avoided looking the assistant in the eye. Jane had already been to the cashpoint to make sure she did not suffer the delay of writing a cheque or using a credit card. Quickly it was all over, she was back in the 2CV and heading towards Harvestdown. Behind her in the footwell was the carrier containing the cookbook, the herb book and another volume called *Making the Most of Your Sex Life*. There was, after all, no point in preparing oneself by going on the pill and then being uncertain what to do next.

At last it was Sunday. Preparations were complete and the time was approaching twelve thirty. Jane caught her breath with excitement as she heard a car scrunching into the drive beside the house. She stepped outside the door to greet her guest. There he stood beside the car, even more perfect, thought Jane, than she had remembered. His craggy features breaking happily with his broad smile, which stretched right up to the corners of his dark eyes. And the car! What a car! A Jaguar, certainly, but not today's model.

"3.8 Mark II, 1960," Tim explained with pride, "Had it restored and rebuilt by a specialist firm. It is now completely as new, probably better."

Jane stroked the gleaming bonnet, dark green, dust-free and without blemish, in awe.

Tim grinned. "I'm glad you like it. It's the love of my life."

Jane laughed. They went inside. So the car was the love of his life. Jane hoped she could cope with this unexpected rival. At least, according to her book, she could do things for him that the car, hopefully, could not. For his part, Tim was pleasantly surprised by Jane's new and more glamorous appearance. She had not been able to maintain quite the level of cosmetic adornment she received at the beauty salon, but they had sent her away with a carrier bag full of expensive creams, foundations, powders and an impressive kit of brushes and pencils of all sizes which appealed to Jane the artist. Today she had made a special effort with all this equipment, but taking care not to overdo it.

Tim was perceptive enough to see her good looks at their previous meetings, but in his own mind had used the adjective *neglected* to describe her to himself. There was now a new confidence and pride, an effort to please, perhaps, which he found both attractive and flattering. There was nothing cheap or flashy about Jane. She wore a pink cotton shirt, blue denim skirt and leather moccasins. Just perfect for the day, thought Tim with approval. It appealed to his sense of order. He wore jeans and a yellow polo shirt. It made them a couple.

The meal was a success. Tim was effusive in his praise. "This is what I call a really good meal", "Just the way I like it" and "God, I wish I could cook like this."

Nevertheless, Jane watched him closely, just in case he was being polite, but she was satisfied that the way he ate proved that he was enjoying it. After lunch they sat in the garden. Throwing caution to the winds, Jane decided to tell him all she knew about the mystery surrounding the manuscript and the cottage. Tim listened intently.

At length Jane concluded, "So I'm going to make arrangements to go to the Isle of Skye and begin the search."

"Do you know the Isle of Skye?"

"No."

"Have you ever been there?"

"No."

"Then let me take you."

Jane nearly collapsed with pleasure, though she fought hard not to show it. "Oh, I couldn't put you to that trouble!"

"It's no trouble. I'd love it. It's one of my favourite places," and moments later, "we should fix dates and make plans."

"Yes," agreed Jane, "let's do it now."

So they went into the kitchen, spread maps on the table and rang directory enquiries for the number of a small hotel which Tim had used before and which he said would be ideal.

"Between Sligachan and Dunvegan, a lovely part which will give us access to the rest of the island without difficulty."

The call was made. Yes, they had rooms. Two singles? They had one single and a double.

"That will do fine. I will fax confirmation in the morning."

He is very businesslike for an author, thought Jane. Writers were supposed to be vague and disorganised.

It was time to make tea. As Jane filled the kettle, she could scarcely believe how well things had gone for her today. They were to set off on Tuesday, stay overnight on the journey and arrive on Wednesday. That would give her tomorrow to close up the house, cancel the newspapers and so on. Jane put the fruitcake on a plate. It should be perfectly mature now. She had not yet cut it because Mitzi did not eat cake when she had come to stay. Jane wondered how Mitzi was. She had had a phone call from her a few days ago, a bit mysterious in some ways. They had agreed to meet again in early August to plan the trip to Venice.

Mitzi then said something rather strange. "When we meet, dear, I have something more to tell you in connection with the events of the past. Something I was not going to mention till later, but I have decided you should know now."

"Can you tell me over the phone?"

"Oh no, dear, but there is no hurry. When we meet will do."

Jane wondered. Something that would help the mystery or deepen it? Tim was on his second piece of cake when the phone rang.

"Miss Block?"

"Yes?"

"Miss Jane Block?"

"Yes?"

It was a man, but she did not recognise the voice. He sounded rather official.

"My name is Humphrey Linnett. You don't know me. I am a solicitor. Specifically, I am Mitzi Feyrbaeme's solicitor."

"Oh!"

Jane was mystified. Why should Mitzi's solicitor be ringing, and on a Sunday, too?

"I'm afraid I have some unfortunate news. Mrs Feyrbaeme was involved in an accident last night. She fell off her bicycle into the path of a van. She has been severely injured. The doctors are becoming pessimistic, but she has been asking for you."

Jane could barely take it in. "Mitzi? I don't believe it. How awful!"

"Could you come at once?"

"Why, yes. Where to?"

"The Accident Hospital in Cambridge."

Jane fought back tears. "I'll set off immediately. It will take some time."

A Gift of Treason

"Come as fast as you can. Go to Reception. I will be waiting." Mr Linnett hung up.

She turned towards Tim, who had detected a crisis and was standing behind her, a look of concern on his face.

"Oh Tim, it's Mitzi Feyrbaeme. She's been in an accident. It's very bad, I must go at once."

He drew her into his arms, where she broke down in sobs.

"Let me drive you. My car is much faster. The 2CV was not designed for an emergency cross-country dash."

Still dabbing her eyes, blowing her nose and doing her very best to pull herself together, Jane sank into the thick leather of the Jaguar, as Tim drove fast and skilfully. It was not until later that she wondered how he could know she had a 2CV, as it was locked in the garage, the doors of which had frosted windows.

The Jaguar sped through the Sunday evening traffic, which at times was quite dense. There were few lorries, although in a car like this Jane felt safe anyway. Tim's driving was both aggressive and fast. At times, they were travelling at over 100 miles per hour. Jane wondered about the police, but Tim seemed confident that he would not be stopped.

He dropped Jane at the entrance to the hospital and set off to park the car. She followed the signs to Reception, and in the waiting area found the solitary figure of Mr Linnett. He was quite short and rather plump, with a round face accentuated by round steel-rimmed spectacles. Evident baldness was disguised by the rudimentary device of combing strands of hair from one side of his head to the other. He wore a tweed jacket and flannels, with a yellow felt waistcoat. This was somewhat blemished by drips of food which had settled on his portly stomach after falling through the gap between spoon and lips. Nevertheless, Jane could detect kindly eyes peering at her from behind the glasses, and his anxious smile was warm and friendly. He hurried towards her.

"Miss Block?"

Jane nodded.

He held out his hand. "Humphrey Linnett. I'm so distressed that we should meet in such circumstances as this. You made wonderful time."

"Yes, a friend drove me. How is Mitzi?"

Mr Linnett shook his head and looked at the floor. "They fear she has not long. Let me take you to her directly. Please follow me, I will show you the way."

Mr Linnett hurried down the passage with short, bouncy steps. Jane followed behind, his image swimming before her as her eyes filled with tears. "Not long..." That meant Mitzi was dying. Jane had little experience of death. Only her mother. That process had been long and slow, with time to adjust. The end, when it came, was a release, a burden lifted, a life enfeebled finally going out like a dying ember. Yet Mitzi, this was sudden and cruel. A life as full and vibrant as any Jane had known, to be forced out when it had so much left to offer. A fall from her bicycle, of all things!

Mr Linnett had stopped outside the Intensive Care Unit. He ushered her towards the doorway. Jane fumbled for her hankie and blew her nose. The ward was small, each bed having its own compartment surrounded by a glazed partition and its banks of monitoring screens and equipment. The paraphernalia to sustain fragile life. There was something especially grim about a natural process being dependent upon machines.

In the third compartment on the left lay a prone figure swathed in bandages connected to wires, tubes and drips. Mr Linnett stopped. A nurse stepped forward from the screens. The solicitor whispered. They beckoned Jane forward. The nurse pulled a chair to the head of the bed.

"Try and talk to her. It may help. Tell her that you're here."

Jane held Mitzi's hand. "Mitzi," her voice came thick and was choked back by more sobs.

Jane struggled to regain control of herself. It had not been like this when her mother died. But now her friend lay dying. Her new friend. A friend whom she had found on her own initiative. She had so few others. Well, only one really, and Celia did not compare with Mitzi. Why should this happen to her? Jane's demands from life were small, why could it not pay without cruel blows?

She tried again. "Mitzi, it's Jane. I'm here beside you, helping you to get better." Jane squeezed Mitzi's hand. She thought she detected a response. "Mitzi? Squeeze my hand if you can hear me."

This time, Jane felt the frail grip tighten perceptibly.

"She knows I'm here," whispered Jane to the nurse.

"Keep talking."

"Mitzi, you are going to be all right, and we'll make that trip to Venice together. You remember how you promised to take me on a gondola in the evening through the little canals and how we are going to sit together at the café in St Mark's Square and have tea and listen to the orchestra?"

Jane felt the grip tighten again, and understood at once that the old lady, looking now so frail and vulnerable, was trying to say something. Jane put her ear close to Mitzi's lips. She heard a feeble whisper, but she heard it well. She drew back and gasped involuntarily, "Mitzi!"

The regular bleep from the heart monitor became a continuous tone. An alarm sounded. The nurse rushed forward.

"Could you please wait outside for a few moments?"

Mr Linnett led her back to the passage where there were some chairs. Two doctors ran past them and disappeared through the swing-doors into the ward.

"I fear this is not good," murmured Mr Linnett.

Jane had stopped crying. She was in a state of shock. Mr Linnett leant towards her.

"As I explained to you over the telephone, I am Mrs Feyrbaeme's solicitor and have been for a number of years. I look after her affairs generally. She has no relatives, or rather, none that she is in contact with. I believe you know she was born in Germany. When she was brought in after the accident yesterday, I came to see her. She was quite lucid. She asked me to tell you that whatever happened, you must make the trip to Skye and solve the mystery of the cottage. On no account were you to delay. The doctors were optimistic at the time, but whilst one recognised that the situation was serious, one had no idea it was grave. Apparently after a good night, she took a turn for the worse at lunchtime. They sent for me, and when I got here and realised how bad things were, I called you."

Jane nodded. "Did she tell you anything about Skye or why I was going there?"

"I'm afraid not. I am just relaying a message exactly as she gave it to me."

The two sat in silence. Eventually the door to the ward opened and one of the doctors appeared, quite young. He invited them into an office across the passage. Jane could tell by his demeanour what he had to say. It could not be easy dealing with relatives at such a time. He said that they had tried everything. They nodded and Mr Linnett said some suitable things about the efforts of the medical staff.

They walked back to the reception area, Mr Linnett holding Jane's arm for comfort. Tim was sitting there, waiting. He rose to greet them. His face was full of concern, but as they approached he could see the answer to his question. Together they led Jane to a seat. The solicitor hurried off to a coffee machine and returned with a steaming cup.

"Sip this. It may help."

Tim and Mr Linnett introduced themselves to each other. Then they stood talking a little out of earshot. Jane drank half the coffee, and then excused herself to the Ladies. When she returned, Mr Linnett stepped forward.

"You will not wish to be bothered with formalities, but I think it would be in order for me just to explain to you that I am Mrs Feyrbaeme's executor. I realise that it is hardly timely to say this, but I feel you should be aware that you are the main beneficiary of her Will."

Jane's red eyes opened wide.

"She changed her Will in your favour very recently. Prior to that the bulk of her estate went to charity. Mrs Feyrbaeme drew my attention particularly to the fact that on her death you may require some special assistance and support. I just want you to know that I regard it as a privilege to carry out her instructions and will be at your disposal at any time."

Jane was confused. She found words difficult. "That's most awfully kind of you. I had no idea Mitzi..." Tears welled up. Tim put his arm around her for comfort.

Mr Linnett continued. "Mr Gulliver tells me that your plans had been laid to go to Skye the day after tomorrow. In view of what I said earlier, I think you should stick to these."

"What about Mitzi's funeral?"

"That can be delayed until your return. There will have to be an inquest in view of the accident, so it would be quite easy to put it off as long as we need to. Nowadays, with, with..." Mr Linnett swallowed a word, perhaps refrigeration, "...with modern methods, delay presents no difficulty."

They shook hands and parted. It was after midnight. Once again, Tim drove at high speed and their progress was rapid as there was less traffic. Mostly they drove in silence. Jane regretted that she had failed to ask for any details of the accident and mentioned this to Tim. Evidently Mr Linnett had explained to him that Mitzi had recently bought a new bicycle, "her old one was a museum piece apparently, but it had a skirt guard over the spokes of the back wheel. The new one did not as nowadays people don't ride bikes in full skirts. Anyway, the frock Mitzi was wearing caught in the back wheel throwing her onto the road near her home right under an approaching delivery van. One of those courier companies, always in a hurry." Jane was dismayed. She even felt that Mitzi might have been persuaded to buy a new bike because of the younger influence of Jane herself. She began to feel guilty.

As the car stopped outside The Hollies, Jane turned to Tim.

Her mind was in turmoil as she tried to focus. "You must be exhausted from all this driving. Please come in and rest." It sounded better than *stay the night*, yet Jane at once regretted her prim decorum.

Inside, Jane made some coffee. It was 3 am. Tim accepted Jane's invitation but refused the spare room and insisted on the sofa. They discussed their plans and agreed that he would set off after three or four hours and return the day after to begin the Scotland trip as originally planned.

"That will give you tomorrow to pack and recover."

Jane nodded. She recognised the romantic opportunity now presented, but was in no condition to take advantage of it and, realizing that Tim was too much of a gentleman to take advantage of her, she made her way up to bed. Alone with her bedroom door shut, she buried her head in her pillow, sobbing. Sobbing not just with grief for her lost friend. Something much worse. There had been no mistaking Mitzi's whisper.

Lucian Feyrbaeme was Jane's father.

CHAPTER ELEVEN

Jane awoke to the sound of a car pulling away. She opened one eye and looked at her bedside clock. It was just after seven. As recollection of events trickled into her mind, she sat up, listening. The house was quiet. She slipped out of bed and onto the landing. She could hear no sound downstairs. The landing window overlooked the front of the house and from this she saw that the Jaguar had gone. Disappointment was added to her feeling of sorrow. She felt awful after so little sleep so she returned to bed, but this was useless as she was wide awake.

All pretence that she was in control of her life was gone. The very foundation upon which it was built, knocked away. The man she thought was her father, her Daddy for whom she was his precious little girl, she could hear those words as if he was speaking them now, was not her father at all. Yet he loved her as his own. Did he know?

Her head throbbing, her mouth thick and her stomach bloated with shock, Jane went through to the kitchen to make some tea. She retrieved her handbag from the hallway where she had left it the night before and took out a photograph. Yes, of course it was obvious. It was not the television personality whom she could see recalled from odd glimpses in teenage years, it was her own face here and now. Alive and clear, caught by a quality camera in a bright shaft of Scottish sun. That was why Trubshaw had sent the image to her. No wonder he talked of a burden. A bombshell!

What now, for God's sake? All the people who could answer her questions, supply the rocks of truth, as a foundation for rebuilding the fabric of her life, were now dead. Lucian, her mother, Daddy, she would always call him that, Trubshaw and now Mitzi, the last hope. Moreover, Mitzi had other things to tell. It was clear to Jane that she had only heard the smallest part of the story. Not her mother's story anymore, upon which she could turn her back if she fancied, or forget. Her own story, her very being. Who she *was*!

There was no doubt about it. She must find the cottage. That would either yield up the secrets or lead her to them. At least there was Tim. Inspector Garlick in person. Certainly the author was as different from the character as chalk from cheese. But he would have the same inquisitive mind. That was the part that counted. Yes. Certainly.

In the sitting room Jane found the blanket she had given to Tim in the small hours, neatly folded it. There was a note.

Did not wake you. Will arrive tomorrow breakfast time. Pack warm clothes and walking boots. I will deal with everything else. Tim

How thoughtful. It would have been just a little better perhaps to end with *Regards*, or *Sincerely* or even *Yours*. But then Tim was not the effusive type, was he? *Love* would have been frivolous. People used the word all the time when they did not mean it. Or even know its true meaning.

Tim had been considerate and attentive. Jane wished so much that she had been more demonstrative. Grief created a great opportunity for comfort, yet she had let it slip by. She suspected Tim was shy with women and was keen to do the right thing. It would offend his ethics to take advantage while she was suffering the trauma of sudden bereavement. Yet she could have snuggled up to him in the car, or just leant her head on his shoulder. She could have held his arm when they got out. She could have sat close to him in the kitchen. There were a hundred little ways in which she could have shown that any attention would be welcome without seeming in any way forward. They had all slipped by. Jane once more broke into sobs. Sobs of frustration and anger, sobs of self-pity, sobs of grief.

Later she pulled herself together and packed for the journey. She called on her neighbours to explain she would be away, and they agreed to keep an eye on the property. Jane cancelled the papers and the milk delivery, threw away uneaten perishables and tidied her studio, arranging it so that she would be able to find everything easily on her return. On her mind all the time were Mitzi's last words. If only Jane could discover more about Diana, Robert and Lucian. It was then that Jane remembered the box.

It was an old leather box in which Diana kept important papers. Birth certificates, insurance policies and so on. There must be a marriage certificate. The box had been consigned to the attic after her mother died. Jane carried a folding ladder from the garage and climbed up to the storage space in the roof, lit dimly by a small skylight. She found the box without difficulty, blew off the dust and returned with it to her studio.

She was right. There was a marriage certificate. This showed that Diana and Robert were married in June 1952. This was only three months before Jane was born. How was it that she had never spotted this? The truth was, of course, that up till now there had been no reason to look.

What did this mean? Robert must have been aware that his future wife was pregnant by someone else. Six months gone, for goodness sake! There was no hiding that!

Had Lucian dumped Diana when he learned of the coming baby? Had he not tried to be a father to his own, and indeed only, child? Had Diana fallen passionately in love with Robert? Somehow that picture did not suit Jane's own surprisingly sharp memory of her parents together. Affection yes, but not the kind of passion that, well…

There was only one thing to be done. Jane would have to ignore her habits and her instincts and allow her life to drift on the many currents and eddies now lapping around it until she came to something solid, where she could set her bearings. Land, as it were, to start again. Although she was in no state for it, she had an adventure beginning tomorrow. With Tim. She must make the best of it. Yes, tomorrow would be the first day of her life adrift.

It was nearly eight when she awoke the next day, having slept like a log. She felt refreshed and more optimistic. An adventure was about to begin. She would be with Tim. His shyness would be bound to wear off, and there would be opportunities after all. Plenty of them. Jane determined to let none slip by. She was just making coffee when she heard the scrunch of tyres on the gravel. Outside she found Tim getting out of his car, but not the Jaguar. Jane stared. A dark green Range Rover loomed high and sinister.

"Where is the Jaguar?"

"It's not really suitable, not where we are going. I borrowed this from a friend. The narrow roads of Skye are not the thing for a precious classic like the Mark Two!"

Tim came forward and kissed her on the cheek. Jane felt comforted and together they went inside for breakfast. Soon the house was locked up and they were on their way. Jane had a bird's-eye view of the countryside from the high vehicle, as once again Tim drove fast, though Jane had no qualms. He seemed instinctively part of his car and in full control. Up the A1 to Scotch Corner, where they crossed the Yorkshire moors and joined the M6 at Penrith. Traffic thinned, the countryside opened, the hills became more majestic and Jane sensed freedom from the overcrowded cosiness of the south. The plan was to drive beyond Stirling to Callander and stop there for the night at the edge of the Highlands.

They found rooms at a rather smart hotel close to the old Roman camp. Jane felt it was extravagant, but Tim insisted on paying. This time he had one of the gold credit cards, which signified extra resources. They had a good dinner and afterwards went to explore the perimeter of the camp marked by banks and mounds. The grass was wet.

"What sort of kit have you brought?" asked Tim.

"Kit?"

"Boots and so on."

"Oh, I brought my hiking boots. They're suede and quite light, and my jeans and some sweaters."

"We'll need to improve on all that."

Jane stopped walking. "Why?"

"If we're going to Skye we must spend some time in the mountains, and we'll need to get you strong boots and waterproofs and things. We must have you properly equipped."

"Mountains? But we're there to look for a cottage."

"You get a good view from the mountains," chuckled Tim.

"But I have no head for heights."

Tim put out his arm and drew her close. "Jane Block, you have been under a lot of pressure and strain. If you are going to see this thing through, whatever it is, you need fresh air and liberation of the spirit. You'll get that from the mountains. Don't worry about the heights, I'll take care of you."

Jane slipped her arm around Tim's waist.

When they returned to the hotel they were thirsty, so Tim suggested a beer in the bar. They sat at a corner table. Jane looked into Tim's eyes. He held her gaze, but upstairs, he gave Jane a goodnight peck on the cheek and disappeared off to his room. Jane closed her own door, disappointed. Some progress had been made today, but it was painfully slow.

Next day, they set off north-west into the Highlands via Crianlarich. Jane had never been this far north before and was enchanted by the remote and rugged mountains, the moors and lochs. After Glencoe they crossed the bridge at Loch Leven, then continued on to Fort William.

Here they found a small hotel by the waterfront and had lunch in the bar. Afterwards, Tim took her to a huge mountain equipment shop. Jane had never seen so many outdoor clothes, rucksacks and boots. Half an hour later, they left with a bag containing a fleece jacket, a pair of water resistant figure-hugging stretch trousers, socks, breathable waterproofs and good leather boots suitable for the rough terrain promised by Tim. He insisted on using the gold card. Jane was torn between thrift and independence. Thrift won.

Back in the Range Rover, they pressed on north and then west at Invergarry on the immortal Road to the Isles. On through spectacular scenery of mountains and glens, they finally reached the Kyle of Loch Alsh. Mid-week the ferry queue was small, so they crossed without delay.

The weather was bright and clear. Jane could not recall having seen such blue water as flowed through the loch, from the shores of which rose the soft green and dappled brown of the hills, capped by scurrying white clouds and azure sky. There was evidence of tourism until Broadford, but after that, Jane and Tim more or less had the road to themselves. Soon they swung in a half circle around the green and red cone of Glamaig.

"That will be your first climb," chuckled Tim. "It's quite safe, a walk really, and from the summit you will be able to see the whole of the island."

Jane craned her neck to study the towering mass and thought it impossible that she would ever get to the top.

At Sligachan they made for Dunvegan, turning off at Struan, down a narrow track, to find their hotel located on a bluff overlooking the beach. As they drew up by the front door, they were faced by a range of grey crags in a solid ridge of mountains, with sharp, basalt slabs reaching high into the sky, their fissures shadowed dark against the rays of the dipping sun. Jane believed she had never seen anything so beautiful.

"Those are the Black Cuillins," murmured Tim, "they are the real mountains."

"Will we go up there?" asked Jane, in a small voice.

"When you're ready," Tim squeezed her hand.

Inside they were welcomed by the proprietress and shown to their rooms. Jane had the double. Dinner would be in an hour.

They sat on stools at the little bar at one end of the dining room. They both sipped whisky, it seemed right, choosing their meal carefully from a robust menu. Jane was content. The day had been a success. Their conversation had been relaxed and animated. They had touched often, a hand here, a nudge there. All very proper, of course, nothing suggestive, but Jane was disappointed that still Tim made no perceptible move. The meal over, a bottle of Beaujolais downed, coffee sipped and finished, their eyes locked once more.

"Let's go for a walk along the beach," said Tim softly.

Before she could stop them, the words flew out of Jane's mouth. "Let's go upstairs," she said.

Later Jane tried to remember the order of events, but her memory was blurred. They left the table at once and in Jane's room they kissed long and deep. She had hardly been kissed before and never like this, neither had she kissed anyone in the way she was now kissing Tim. Gradually their hands began to move. Item by item, clothing dropped to the floor until they fell naked to the bed. Jane lost all self-consciousness in her admiration of his body and the discovery of her own, until at last, in an ecstasy beyond her wildest dreams, she broke the shackles of the lonely barren years and set her body free.

CHAPTER TWELVE

At breakfast, Jane found herself enjoying a new and sharper reality. She watched Tim opposite, spreading marmalade on his toast. Strange how many details, missed before, she could see now. The dark hairs across the back of his hand, curling small beneath the bracelet of his watch. The cheeks of his face stretched taut across the wide bones. The deep brown eyes, passionate but full of mystery. The dark hair, thick and heavy, combed straight back in long sweeps until it twisted into tiny curls at the nape of his neck. The precise way he ate, mouthful by mouthful, leaving a crumbless, jam-free plate. Jane was happy to have no more on her agenda for the day than to sit and watch him.

The toast over, his lips wiped clean with a double flourish of his napkin, he grinned at her and spoke. "Glamaig today. We'll get you acclimatised."

"Glamaig? That huge mountain?"

"Just a hill..."

"Shouldn't we be looking...?"

"We can do that afterwards, but first we must get you fit." He laughed, "You will have sharper eyes after you've conquered Glamaig!"

Jane was none too certain, but she did not care. She did not even care if they abandoned their search altogether, so long as whatever they did she was with him. Dimly she recognised that she was reacting like a teenager, but then, she had never really been a teenager, so perhaps it was better late than never.

Ruby, the waitress, appeared with two small carriers containing their packed lunches and while Jane was changing into her hiking clothes, he was busy packing rucksacks and stowing items into the Range Rover. As they set off, the weather seemed unsettled. The Cuillins were shrouded in mist or low cloud, Jane was not sure which, and although there were patches of blue here and there, rain threatened.

"Is the weather right for this sort of thing?" she asked uncertainly.

Tim looked at her. "It is not ideal, but this is an island and the weather is very changeable. It even varies from one part of the island to another. If we were going up the Black Cuillins, I would hesitate, particularly with an inexperienced companion. But Glamaig is part of the Red Cuillins, much gentler hills, grass covered mostly, where there is no risk. I know them well so we will not get lost."

Jane recognised the futility of protest. "Will we be able to see anything at the top?"

"I hope the weather will clear. It should be kind to you as a newcomer on the summit and give you your reward."

Jane smiled to herself. She would have to get used to the fact that she would not be able to change the mind of her lover once it was made up. No matter, she hated indecision. She slid across the seat and leant on Tim's shoulder as he drove.

As the road crested the hill above Sligachan, patches of sunshine dappled the sides of Glamaig and its summit was visible. Shortly, Tim stopped at a lay-by on the shore of the loch. He opened the tailgate catch. A small, soft ball flew through the air and Jane caught it. It turned out to be a pair of black silk socks.

"Take your boots off and slip them onto your feet next to your skin. They won't take up any room, but if you wear thick socks over them you will be free of blisters and sore toes."

Jane sat down on the ground and did as she was told. When she was ready Tim handed her a rucksack. It was larger than the flimsy affair she used on the Downs.

"In here are waterproofs, your packed lunch, water, a spare sweater, a woolly hat and two chocolate bars."

Heavens, thought Jane. She put the pack on her back. It seemed quite heavy.

"Do I have to carry this up there?" She looked at the cone looming before her, blotting out the sun.

"Yes, the mountain rescue people get very angry when they are called out to retrieve hikers in trainers and T-shirts. Here, put this in your pocket. If we get separated for some reason, give it three long blasts and repeat after a minute."

Jane stared at the whistle in the palm of her hand. She began to feel quite nervous. She had no idea it was going to be anything like this. Tim had locked the doors and was crossing the road. She looked at his long legs and lean figure, and recalled his nakedness as they had made love again when they awoke that morning.

She hurried after him through a gateway and across the gently sloping uneven ground towards the base of the hill. Steeper and steeper it became, but although puffing, Jane found their progress exhilarating. Eventually it was so steep that Jane found if, when standing, she stretched a hand in front of her face, it touched the rising ground which rose endlessly to the sky. They worked diagonally back and forth. Tim called it traversing. He made Jane move ahead, so that he was behind and below her. This gave her confidence. Now and again she looked back. The Range Rover was becoming quite tiny, and she could see the blue outline of the loch as it stretched towards the narrows that separated Skye from the tiny island of Raasay.

Jane began to wonder whether she could cope with the height, but Tim encouraged her onward. At length, they traversed the shoulder of the hill and came upon a slope of tight turf grazed smooth by mountain sheep, which wound upwards but was less steep. The summit appeared to be in reach. Jane struggled on. At last she stood embracing Tim beside the cairn which marked the top, buffeted by the strong wind and ecstatic at the unparalleled view in all directions, which enabled them to see every part of the island from shore to shore.

"I told you that the weather would reward you for the effort!"

Jane answered by kissing him full and deep.

"How far have we climbed?"

"Just over two thousand eight hundred feet. We started at sea level. Unlike mountains in some places where you drive up part of the way, here on Skye, you always begin at sea level and climb every foot."

Jane sighed. How her life had changed. And so quickly! Maybe to drift was the right approach to life.

They found a spot in the lea of the wind to eat their sandwiches. Tim showed her the map.

"Instead of going straight down the way we came up, we'll descend the southern slope to the pass," it was marked on the map in Gaelic, "and then swing north-west down the slopes to the Sligachan Hotel."

Looking at the map Jane was not daunted by the prospect. She loved the names and she could see the route made a complete circle.

"Are these smaller hills part of Glamaig?" she asked.

"Well, they're connected to it. Such hills are often known as outriders."

Tim produced binoculars from his rucksack and Jane watched the tiny ferry crossing from Raasay. She wondered if they could make love out here in the open. Perhaps not. The air was far from warm and although they seemed to be alone, that might be an illusion caused by the scale of things. Others, too, might have binoculars. It would never do to titillate anonymous peeping eyes. Or would it? To her dismay, Jane momentarily found the idea exciting. She shivered and began stuffing oddments into her rucksack.

"Shall we make a move?"

Tim hesitated. Jane wondered. Was he thinking the same? At length he smiled. "Yes, I think we'd better."

It was late afternoon by the time they reached the car. The return had required two quite significant climbs and a walk of some miles, at times over rough and difficult ground. Jane was physically exhausted, though her mind was sharp and her spirit uplifted. The journey appeared to have had no effect whatever on Tim, who opened the tailgate and after rummaging produced a flask.

"Hot tea slightly sweetened. It will buck you up."

They sat on the shore of the loch, sipping and munching biscuits. The sun shone continuously now. The gulls swooped and dived, their wistful cries echoing through the hills. Jane decided that this was the best day of her life. Tim put his arm around her. As she looked up at his bronzed features framed by the blue of the sky, her heart was so full of feeling that she could not express it. Although she wanted to say something, in the end she said nothing. He leant forward and kissed her softly on the lips.

"We should drive down to Broadford now and see if we can spot our cottage in that section of the island, although I think it is unlikely that is where they would have chosen."

"Why?" asked Jane.

"It's too close to the mainland. Although in the forties and fifties there were many fewer visitors, I suspect Lucian and your mother would have found somewhere more secluded."

It was half past seven by the time they returned to the hotel, having combed Broadford and the country between there and Sligachan. Of the doorway with the antlers there was no sign. After a hurried shower and a change, they were seated for dinner shortly after eight.

There was something Jane had to know. She felt now was the time. Yet the meal was over and they were sitting alone in the lounge before she finally asked.

"Have you ever been married?"

Tim looked up. There was a pause.

"I wondered if you would ask. The answer is yes and no."

"How do you mean?"

"I had a live-in partner for ten years. We decided to get married. We went to the Bahamas to stay with her brother who lived out there. One afternoon he took her scuba diving. She had some experience but not enough. She became entangled in some nets caught on a wreck not far from the shore. Neither of them was carrying a knife. I think she panicked.

He swam back for help. It reached her too late. I was a bit of a mess for some time after. Eventually it all became history, but nothing much happened after that on the romantic front."

Jane put her hand on Tim's. "I am desperately sorry. I should never have asked."

"Not at all. You have a right to know." Tim leant forward and kissed her gently on the lips. Jane thought she could sense an echo of pain. An echo from history maybe, but there nevertheless.

Later as she lay in the arms of her sleeping lover, Jane felt a slight disappointment that she had not been asked about her amorous past.

It must be obvious that there was none.

CHAPTER THIRTEEN

Over the following days their programme fell into a pattern. When the weather was fine and clear, they walked the hills and mountains, achieving three ascents in the Black Cuillins. Jane found these nerve-racking. Friendly grass was replaced by rock. Some of this was shattered and sharp, some smooth, slippery and treacherous. Elsewhere she found it rough and abrasive, tearing tiny cuts in the skin of her hands. Nevertheless she managed heights and slopes that only two weeks ago she would have considered quite impossible.

When the weather was overcast or raining, which was often, they tramped the coastal paths and beaches, so deserted that they speculated it could have been a year or more since another human had passed that way. They saw the mournful, abandoned ruins of little crofts and villages, their inhabitants driven from their heritage, many to sail overseas to achieve fame and fortune in new civilizations. The simple evidence of their roots formed weather-beaten memorials to the old way of life, now gone and all but forgotten.

Always the pair returned to the Range Rover in the afternoon and set off to different parts of the island in a vain search for the antlers over the doorway. Jane came to regard the quest as hopeless.

"It is worse than trying to find a needle in a haystack. The antlers have probably rotted and fallen off their mounting, or a new owner has taken them down. We could have passed the place several times and not recognised it. To identify the correct doorway, even if it has not been altered after all these years, we depend upon the purest luck. It may not even be on this island. After all, the fish box is our only clue and it may be false. Even your Inspector Garlick would be hard pressed. And he's pretend. We're real!"

Tim laughed. "Don't worry. Even in haystacks needles can be found if you search long enough." Jane tried to keep a grip of common sense, but found herself caught by Tim's optimism.

Then on the eleventh day, because the morning was wet, they made a visit to Dunvegan Castle, seat of the Macleods. Tim and Jane toured the historic rooms and saw where Dr Johnson was said to have been given hospitality. They walked the beautiful gardens in which water, hardly surprising in so damp a climate, was a major feature, before taking a short boat trip to a tiny offshore island in the loch to see the dozens of grey seals basking on the rocks, bewhiskered, puffing and ungainly. After they had eaten their picnic in the Range Rover to keep dry from the rain, the clouds dispersed and the warm sun beat down through the sharp, clear air.

Tim had the map spread across his knees. He suggested that as the weather had improved, they drive around the western shore of the loch up to a tiny community called Galtrigill and then walk the last mile or so to Dunvegan Head.

"We shall be on top some of the highest cliffs in the British Isles. The drop to the sea is nearly a thousand feet."

Jane was a touch reluctant. Her desire for Tim drove her to wonder whether it would be better to return to the hotel. But his sense of adventure was infectious and they set off, turning south of Dunvegan along a narrow road which gave spectacular views of the castle projecting from the opposite shore of the loch. At length the twisting, bumpy lane came to an end by a bungalow and an older croft. Tim parked the car and they plodded on foot through rough and soggy ground towards the clifftop. The going was heavy. Water coursing through the peat cut deep and invisible gullies into which an unwary foot could plunge thigh-deep, toppling the unsuspecting walker face down in the heather. This happened once to Jane, but no harm was done and they both laughed.

The cliff was reached without further mishap, and they crawled on their stomachs to the edge, peering down through wispy cloud which floated beneath them, to the churning waters below. They watched diving cormorants and swooping gulls, heard the shriek of oyster catchers and felt the tang of the salt air of the sea on their cheeks. Beyond the sight of the cottages, and quite alone but for the birds, they kissed passionately until Jane drew him to her, crying out in celebration of her love for this man and the towering majesty of their clifftop union.

They walked back down the slope towards the car arm in arm. Suddenly, as the cottages came into view, Jane stopped.

"Have you your binoculars?"

"Yes."

"Let me have them. Quickly."

Tim delved into his rucksack. Jane held the glasses to her eyes.

"There they are!"

"What?"

"The antlers! Above the doorway of that croft! We missed it coming up because the door was to the side, and therefore behind us as we walked!" She threw her arms around Tim. "We've done it! It's exactly as the photograph. We have found the cottage! I had given up hope. This is just unbelievable!" Jane's voice shook with excitement and emotion. She fought back tears of joy.

Tim took the glasses. "You're right!"

Hand in hand they ran now, bouncing over the rough ground. They reached the doorway. Nervously Jane knocked. There was no answer. Tim tried the door. It was open. They both stood on the threshold peering in.

A female voice in broad Scottish, behind them called, "I've been waiting for you. Mr McAllister said you would be coming."

They turned. Hurrying up the path was a short woman, with strands of disordered mousy hair above a weather-beaten face bearing witness to the harsh and unrelenting life of a modern crofter. But her eyes were bright. Jane, caught at once by those eyes, thought they reflected an inner contentment. A contentment of the soul.

"You'll find everything perfect. All these years I have kept it just the same. Except now there is the electric, and two years ago Mr Trubshaw had the Calor gas for the heating done and threw out the old peat range."

Jane stepped forward. "I'm afraid I don't have any of the details."

"Ah, you'll not be bothered." The little woman extended her hand. "I'm Kirsty MacFee. You'll be Jane? Angus, my husband he is, and I run the holding and keep some sheep. We can have the profits from that, and Mr Trubshaw, well now the poor soul has died, the agent, Mr McAllister, pays us an annual fee to look after the main property. We have the bungalow," she pointed to a more modern structure nearby, "rent free."

"Ah," said Jane.

"You'll want to look around. Come and see me if you want to know anything, but I'll let you alone just now."

Jane and Tim nodded their thanks.

"It sounds as if it's not just a cottage but a smallholding. A real croft," said Jane excitedly.

"Come on," said Tim, "let's go inside."

Jane swung back the door. They stood in the kitchen. Quite spacious, simply furnished with a scrubbed table, probably deal, and four chairs in the centre with an old-fashioned dresser with plates standing upright and hanging cups. The sink had been renewed at some stage and was of stainless steel with cupboards underneath.

The doorway led through to the living room. This was bright with two windows and ran the length of the little building. There was an arch in the middle, suggesting that once it would have been two. There were armchairs, a sofa, an oak bureau with a top that opened back to form a writing platform and a glass-fronted cabinet containing tumblers and wineglasses. In the corner was a door which opened onto a narrow flight of stairs leading to the first floor. Here there were two bedrooms of quite good size. There was no sign of a bathroom, but they found this later through the kitchen.

Everything was spotlessly clean, and the row of horse brasses which hung from the crossbeam of the large open fireplace was bright from frequent polishing. The smell of scented furniture wax hung in the air. Jane sat in an armchair, looking around her silently, too emotional to speak. These walls knew the secrets of her mother's annual liaison with Lucian, how Robert Block came into the picture and why Lucian abandoned his pregnant lover and her unborn child. Would they now yield those secrets to Jane herself, almost certainly conceived within their protection?

Tim had opened the top of the bureau. "Here's what you're looking for," he said softly, turning.

He held an envelope sealed with wax. Tim handed it to Jane. She could make out the imprint of a crest, as she broke the seal with her finger. Inside she found the deeds to the property. To Jane's surprise these were in her own name and had been since 1952, the year she was born.

She looked up as Tim spoke again. "And there is this."

It was the manuscript. The top page bore its title, *The Hastings Option by Lucian Feyrbaeme*. It was typed on an old-fashioned typewriter with small letters. The pages were packed tight with text. Jane set it down on the low table in front of the sofa.

Here then, was the account of past treachery. In these pages was the story of treason conspired, of traitors hovering in the wings of a nation's anguish, returning to the cover of respectability when defeat was averted, to continue as pillars of the very establishment which in cowardice they planned to betray. For this sheaf of words survivors or descendants of the guilty were evidently prepared to burgle, to threaten and, Jane barely dared think it, perhaps even to kill.

Jane turned to the first page. It was headed *Author's Note* but the text was quite short:

In 1940, when Great Britain stood alone, all her European allies having succumbed to the might of the victorious forces of Nazi Germany, when the nation faced the very real prospect of defeat, a group of senior civil servants, politicians and members of the armed forces, conspired together that if it were certain that a German invasion was imminent, they would overthrow the Churchill Government, seize power and make peace.

The plotters called themselves and their plan "The Hastings Option", harking back to the Norman Conquest a millennium earlier, in which they argued that, though conquered, England had absorbed the invader and gone on to become the greatest imperial power the world had ever seen. They persuaded themselves that the imperial prospect of Anglo-German unity far outshone Churchill's plan to fight to oblivion, when a vanquished and shattered country would be ground beneath the heels of a triumphant and vengeful enemy.

This book is the story of that plan. It charts what might have happened and identifies all the key plotters. I can vouch for its accuracy because I was numbered by the plotters as one of their kind, yet in their treachery, I was their traitor. When I reported unfolding events to the authorities, no action was taken, as if their competence was ebbing with the adverse tide of war. Later, when that tide turned, still no action was taken. The fabric of national unity was preserved so that in victory, the steadfast people could celebrate that unity of national achievement, unsullied by whispers of traitors in their midst.

Many of these plotters and their families prospered in the post-war era, sustained their positions of leadership and rose higher still, were honoured and revered. I began to feel that the history of Great Britain in the twentieth century could never rise above the level of propaganda unless this stark chapter saw the light of day. Yet in a final act of personal cowardice which puts me on the level of those I accuse, I have directed that this manuscript should form that part of my estate which will be inherited, by my companion and partner on this island during many happy summers, twenty years after my death, or on her prior death, to our daughter Jane Block, and I leave it to their determination and judgement as to whether, in the context of a modern world, this account should break into the public domain.

Skye 1965

Jane leant back into the cushions of the sofa. Her mind was spinning.

Tim looked at her. "May I read?" She handed him the sheet. "So Feyrbaeme was your father," Tim said at length. He nodded to himself. "I guessed as much. This whole drama was too much to be just a leftover from a long ago affair of your mother's. And," Tim smiled, then kissed Jane tenderly on the forehead, "there is another thing. You look very like that photo of him!"

Jane nodded. "I only found out from Mitzi's last words. That's why I was in such a state. I still am deep down, but I hope to find some answers here." She waved her hand in a gesture drawing the room into an intimacy with her. "Now I am here, I feel everything I want to know is in this cottage."

Tim took her in his arms. They did not kiss. They were gripped in an affectionate embrace. That was all, at this moment, Jane needed. Then she whispered, "Let's go now and see Mrs MacFee".

They walked to the bungalow and both were soon seated at the table in a warm and homely kitchen. It was probably the largest room in the bungalow and, as is often the case when the inhabitants spend their time out of doors, was obviously the main living room. There was a rocking chair in front of the peat burning range, on which a kettle sang.

"We have a gas boiler now for hot water and three radiators, fed by the same butane tank as the house. It's free, thanks, I suppose," her blue eyes twinkled, "to you," Mrs MacFee spoke as she handed Jane her tea.

Jane hesitated. "Mrs MacFEE, I'm afraid I don't really know the details of the arrangements here. Mr Trubshaw died before he was able to give them to me. Indeed, I had no idea where the property was and came upon it quite by chance."

"Really?" said Mrs MacFee, "Mr McAllister said Mr Trubshaw had sent you all the details before he died."

"No," said Jane, "unfortunately he managed only to invite me to visit him, but he died before we met."

"Oh dear," Mrs MacFee shook her head, "I don't think Mr McAllister knew that. Of course, Mr Trubshaw was known to be very frail. That's why he gave up coming up here."

"Coming up here?"

"Yes, he used to come up every year to check on the property and arrange for improvements, but as I said before, when he got too ill, he engaged Mr McAllister as his agent."

"Who is Mr McAllister?"

"Well, he's none too young either. He must be in his seventies. He lives north of Portree on the East Coast. He owns a tidy bit of property on the island rented out for holiday lets. I think that's why Mr Trubshaw engaged him."

"Mrs MacFee, did you meet Lucian Feyrbaeme?"

"No, not that I remember. Mr Feyrbaeme and, er, your mother, bought the croft just after the war. They used to come here once a year for a long holiday, most of July and August. Sometimes even a bit of September. My parents rented the land from them. We lived in a little place just down the road. When they stopped coming here regularly, Mr Feyrbaeme decided he wanted the property permanently looked after and kept in a proper state. So he built the bungalow and arranged with my parents to be caretakers. I told you, he paid a fee, which was very welcome, the profit from the crofting being what it is. In those days I was only a wee bairn.

"Later, when I grew up and married Angus, we lived in Carbost by the distillery where my husband worked. Then my father died, and shortly afterwards Angus lost his job, so we took over the croft and the caretaking. This was after Mr Feyrbaeme himself had died. We've only ever dealt with Mr Trubshaw and Mr McAllister."

"And your mother?"

"She lives in a home now in Inverness. I'm afraid her mind has gone. She doesn't even know who we are."

"I'm sorry," murmured Jane, "that must be awful. How many acres are there?"

"Twenty-five."

"Do you grow anything?"

"No, just a few vegetables. The climate and ground are not right for crops. We have the sheep and two or three highland cattle for milk and calving. We sell the young ones." Mrs MacFee poured more tea. "I'm sure you don't want to be bothered with this now, but we are your tenants." Mrs MacFee looked nervous. "You must tell us if you want to make any changes."

Jane was quick. "I want everything to remain exactly as it is. I shall obviously want to spend time here, but my home is in the south, so it would be very good if you are willing to continue. I shall, of course, continue the fee."

Mrs MacFee nodded with relief.

As they walked back to the little house, Jane wondered where the money came from to pay the fee. Presumably Lucian must have left funds in the hands of Trubshaw. Now that Trubshaw was dead, what happened to these and where were they? It was now after six. Jane felt exhausted by the emotion of the day.

"Let's leave the manuscript as it is, here. It's quite safe, and come back tomorrow and start reading."

"We can start reading tomorrow, certainly," responded Tim, "but I suggest we take it with us."

"It's been safe here all this time."

"I know, but one does not want to take chances. And there's another thing."

"What's that?" asked Jane anxiously.

"Well, you heard Mrs MacFee say that the agent thought that Trubshaw had given you all the details, yet his housekeeper knew nothing about it and certainly nobody has been in touch with you since. For example, solicitors and so on."

"What are you getting at?"

"Maybe the burglar who broke into Trubshaw's house did find something and took it. That means he or the people he represents knows as much, possibly more, than we do."

A shiver of fear ran up Jane's spine. Tim was right. She would keep the manuscript with her at all times.

Back at the hotel, Tim and Jane had a celebratory drink. Their search, which had seemed so hopeless, had suddenly borne fruit. A part of Jane's life from which she had been disconnected had become a reality. Yet instead of feeling elated, overjoyed even, Jane felt weary, nervous and perhaps frightened. What was she going to read in those pages? Would they identify the person or people by whom she felt threatened? Should she publish, or were those events too long ago, with the traitors, like Lucian, dead? The nation had written its history. Would it not be best to let the record stand and let this murky chapter be covered by the sands of time, since it was now too late for knowledge of these things to do any good?

She put her thoughts to Tim at dinner in a low voice reduced at times to a whisper. He looked at Jane with steady eyes.

"Until you have read the manuscript you can't answer that."

By the time they had finished dinner, Jane was too sleepy to start reading, so they agreed to leave the manuscript untouched until morning. They went to bed early, but she had fallen asleep before lovemaking got beyond the cuddling stage.

Next morning they had an early breakfast. Jane suggested they return to the croft with the manuscript and read it there. By ten o'clock they were sitting together on the sofa with the densely typed pages before them. As they were loose, it was possible for Jane to read a page, then pass it to Tim, so that they progressed together with Tim never more than a page behind.

To begin with, Jane was not sure that she was interested in what she was going to read, or cared that much about it, but as she read her mood changed from apathy to interest, and then to dismay. The plotters included four quite senior members of the government, though none in the War Cabinet, senior officers from all three services and top civil servants. The leading plotters formed what they called the Grand Committee, and it was here that the strategic planning took place. No one knew how many others were influenced, directly or indirectly, by these people, but it was probably hundreds. Evidently, through high level contacts in Lisbon, terms had already been agreed with the Germans.

There was a considerable benefit if the plotters were able to gain power through pulling the strings of Britain's limited democratic machine before the invasion was launched. In that event Great Britain would be left entirely independent and unscathed, provided a free hand was given to Germany in Europe. In return we would keep our Empire. There would be no humiliation and Britain's undefeated status would be recognized in the peace treaty.

If the plotters failed to get into power before the invasion was launched, they would use their deep penetration of the fabric of command and control, as soon as a German bridgehead was established, to start a programme of gentle disintegration. Orders would be delayed. Ammunition would be slow to arrive, or to the wrong points. Air cover would arrive late and in the wrong place, causing the troops to become demoralised and reduce their fighting spirit. The supposed benefit of this would be less resistance with a reduction in casualties.

At a certain point, designated in the plan as *H Hour*, organised to coincide with a meeting of the War Cabinet, Churchill and his key ministers would be sealed in the underground bunker where they always held their meetings at that time, and their communications cut off. They would be held out of touch in this way for twenty-four hours, during which The Hastings Option would seize the reigns of power, call for a cease-fire and open negotiations with the Germans. In response, The German High Command, who had knowledge of the plan, would ensure that German forces avoided excesses against the civilian population. This would make armistice arrangements more popular. Waffen SS divisions and Gestapo units would be held in the rear, leaving, for the moment unmolested, refugees who had fled to Britain from the various parts of conquered Europe. This concession would exclude German nationals and Jewish refugees.

Churchill and his Cabinet would then be arrested and held in custody until an armistice was signed. After that they would be offered pardons in exchange for swearing allegiance to the New Order. If they refused, they would be arrested for treason, for which the penalty would be death. London would be declared an open city, and German forces would be allowed to advance north to the Midlands, stopping at a line across the country from the Wash to Cardigan Bay. South of this would be the occupied zone, initially under the authority of the German military governor, but north of this line the country would be free of enemy forces and governed from York, which would become the capital of a puppet government.

Both the plotters and the Germans favoured retention of the British monarchy, but it was expected that the King, and certainly the Queen, would refuse to cooperate. The crown would be offered to the former King, now Duke of Windsor, whose pro-German views had worried the Baldwin government as much as Wallis Simpson and who, as he kept saying, was mostly German anyway.

Initially he would rule from York where he would be crowned, having abdicated before his previous coronation, but with far wider powers than his deposed brother. Democracy would be adjusted to a more autocratic mode in which the power of the civil service and military would be in the ascendant. Mosely would get something, but he was not highly regarded so it would be a lot less than he would expect.

The plotters hoped to achieve more favourable terms in a peace treaty than those meted out to Vichy France, as they saw synergy between the two Protestant powers. They hoped also that the German occupation would be short-lived. They saw a vague future of a united Anglo-German nation dominating the continent through the German military and controlling much of the rest of the world with the resources of the British Empire and the Royal Navy. In due course the objective would be to apply this combined might to the destruction of Communist Russia.

If the plotters failed to overthrow Churchill and his government, either because their plot failed or because they lacked the will to launch it, the Germans believed they would conquer without difficulty. They would then exact total surrender. The country would be occupied, the population enslaved or starved and all its wealth and resources plundered. Himmler's entire fiendish apparatus would be given free reign.

It was obvious to any student of modern history that such schemes would have appealed to Hitler and his headstrong followers, but it was indeed a shock to find that an important section of the British Establishment, however small, was prepared to engineer the defeat of its own country. It was the success of the RAF in the Battle of Britain that caused the plotters to miss their opportunity to replace the Churchill government by, what would appear as, legitimate means and as the German invasion never happened after that, the opportunity for the coup was never there. Later, when the war took a different course there was a further attempt to organize peace involving Rudolf Hess. Much the same people were involved but this time Churchill was ready and out maneuvered them.

The names were there, all the key ones, including countless references to Flemington, Celia's current surname. It was evident from the text that the key government member in the plot was Monty's grandfather.

Lucian devoted several pages to this family. It appeared that Monty's mother was the daughter of a high ranking Nazi who had fled to Argentina with his family at the end of the war and made a fortune under the patronage of the Peron regime. In a remarkable act of defiance this former SS Colonel had sent his daughter to an English finishing school, from which she had drifted into that part of society which was willing quietly to accept right-wing connections. In due course, she met Monty's father, the son of the most senior would-be traitor in Churchill's government, who could see the advantages of her fortune and who evidently felt that a sufficient smokescreen had been put up in Argentina to avoid connection with Germany. So they were married, shortly before the new bridegroom followed in his father's footsteps and was elected to Parliament. Monty was the only child of the marriage.

This explained both the financial security to which Celia had referred and the sightings of Monty in odd places. Was Monty the burglar who caused Trubshaw's death? Exactly what Monty was doing or what his plan was, Jane could not yet tell, but at least his background explained some of the mystery, if not all. It was obvious what Monty was after, but how had he heard about it in the first place? Why had he started to search exactly twenty years after Lucian's death, and when Jane was sent the photo? If it was that important, why had he not carried out his search five years earlier, or at some other time? Why wait until now? Was it a coincidence that he was married to Jane's best friend? Was that chance? Or had Celia been brought into the plot? She hardly had a head for such things. Beautiful, yes, but brains... well, at school she had been bottom in everything and failed most of her exams.

It was odd that although Monty had spied on Jane's meeting with Tim at The Speaker's Arms and may have followed her to Cairo, he was nowhere to be seen up here. Jane asked Tim for his opinion, but he appeared rather out of his depth. He suggested that Monty may work for some government agency, perhaps the Secret Service. He pointed out that this would tie up with his vague duties at the Foreign Office.

"Surely if the government were involved, they would be more straightforward than this," Jane remarked.

Tim shook his head. "From all I read, the secret services are a law unto themselves. It is they who would be the most heavily criticized if you publish this."

Jane shuddered. In spite of everything so far, the reality was more frightening than she had expected. It took them two days to complete the reading, at the end of which Jane was exhausted by the enormity of what she had seen and weighed down by the responsibility for the decision that Lucian had left her. It made sense to return to England now. Tim came up with the idea of taking the manuscript to Mr Linnett, who could arrange for a bank to keep it in the strongroom. They would pass close to Cambridge on their way down the M11, so it would be a small detour.

Jane found the last dinner at the hotel sombre and depressing. The weather had closed in. A cold wind blew from the north-west and rain beat upon the panes of the dining room. She had the worry of the manuscript on her mind and was still somewhat in a state of emotional shock following the discovery of the croft. There was much in it that she had not yet seen, but it made her parents real people to her. What was not yet clear was the involvement of Robert Block, whose name she bore and whom she still thought of as her father.

Another worry was Tim. Jane was now quite certain she was in love with him, but she was uncertain of his feelings. With men, sex and love did not have to go hand in hand. He was passionate, yes, but the passion was physical. Love was emotional. She sought for evidence of emotion, but she could find nothing beyond tenderness. Was that enough? She was not sure what was going to happen when they returned home. He had not said anything. Were they to kiss and part? Was this just a holiday romance? Was this the end of her completeness? If only he would speak of it. She could speak first, but that may drive him away. They made love that night, but Jane was not in the mood and she lay afterwards, tossing, sleepless, unfulfilled.

Jane wanted to leave early and Tim drove as fast as traffic and highland roads would permit. They could have completed the journey in a day, but would have passed Cambridge after office hours, which would have made contacting Mr Linnett difficult. Tim suggested they stay the night in York, so they spent a pleasant enough evening in that historic city. Jane wondered what the inhabitants would say if they knew that their town might, but for the turn of history, have become the capital of the traitorous government of a betrayed nation.

At last Tim raised the question of what should happen next. Strolling near the floodlit Minster, he turned to her.

"What are your plans?"

Jane was not sure.

"I have some personal business to attend to, so I need a few days to myself," said Tim. "But why don't I come down and fetch you on Friday so that we can spend the weekend together, this time at my house? There are some things I'd like to talk to you about."

What a relief!

"Yes," said Jane, "I would like that." She took Tim's arm and held tight, yet her grip was only part affection. Mostly fear. Of what she did not yet know.

CHAPTER FOURTEEN

Tim telephoned ahead to make an appointment to see Mr Linnett at midday. They bought a large envelope and sealed the manuscript inside. Jane described it as documents related to her mother, of some value, which might attract thieves. Mr Linnett, who had already been alerted by Mitzi before she died to expect unusual calls for assistance, took it all in his stride.

"I shall place them in my safe directly, and this afternoon transfer them to the strongroom of my firm's bank. You can rest assured that they will be absolutely secure."

It was timely to discuss the arrangements for Mitzi's funeral. Mr Linnett rang the undertakers and arranged it for the following week. A private cremation with as little fuss as possible. Mr. Linnett seemed aware of Jane's anguish.

"There was a memorial service at King's Chapel for her late husband, to which all the academic and literary notables came. I am sure I could arrange something similar for Mrs. Feyrbaeme later, if you wished. It would be very well attended. Meanwhile I will designate the cremation private." He looked at Jane. "*Strictly* private," he added with emphasis.

Tim waited until they were back in the car before suggesting to Jane that she extend her stay at the weekend, so that he could drive her up on the Tuesday morning for the funeral.

"Funerals are always upsetting and I can bring you comfort."

Jane kissed his cheek. The event might be sad, but the portents looked happy. So it was that Jane became more relaxed and at peace as their journey to Sussex drew to its close. She was excited by the invitation to visit Tim's house at the weekend and it was a relief to know that the manuscript was safe. Mr Linnett seemed most helpful. Just the sort of person upon whom Jane felt she could rely. The quest for her heritage had been successful, and she now owned a delightful retreat which was full of the trinkets of her past, which she would have ample time to enjoy.

There were still elements of the mystery to unravel, and menace lurked not far away, but with Tim to protect her and a greater understanding of her background, Jane felt she could cope. True, she had to decide whether to publish Lucian's account of the wartime treachery. It would be an advantage to get it out of the way and the money was tempting. On the other hand it would open old wounds, or worse, wounds which had remained covered and unseen. The harsh glare of publicity would shine upon her. Jane wondered if she was too private a person to withstand what she knew might become the ravages of the media. Her whole life could be ruined.

But the old life of isolation and retreat had gone. Not because it had been snatched away. Jane herself had suddenly grown out of it. She wanted more than before, but not perhaps as much as was available.

After Tim had dropped her at the cottage, staying only for a quick cup of tea and an affectionate embrace, Jane cooked herself an omelet and unpacked her suitcase. She then settled down to watch the news on television. "I will collect you on Friday evening in the Jaguar" were Tim's last words as they parted. Just as well, thought Jane afterwards, as she had forgotten to ask him for his address. She only had his phone number.

Jane jumped at the sudden jangle of her front door bell. Nervously she opened the door to the front porch. There two men stood. Stocky, grey suited, with short hair.

The elder of the two, who cannot have been more than thirty, stepped forward and asked, "Miss Jane Block?"

Jane nodded, her pulse racing and her stomach churning. He opened an identity wallet in the palm of his hand.

"Sergeant Bowers and Constable North. We are from Special Branch."

Jane was incredulous. "Special Branch?"

The sergeant nodded. "Would you please accompany us, Miss Block?"

Jane's knees went weak. "At this hour?"

"I'm afraid so, it is important."

"Where to?"

"Not far."

"I'm not sure." Jane hesitated. "Supposing I refuse?"

The two men stared at her and said nothing.

"Let me just get a coat and turn off the television."

At a nod from Sergeant Bowers, Constable North followed Jane into the house and stood watching as she took her coat from the cupboard in the hall. She stood, uncertain.

"I shall be back tonight?"

The young man nodded.

Outside was a small saloon car. They put her in the back seat and drove off at speed. Jane was in turmoil. Was she being kidnapped? Was there such a thing as Special Branch? How could she tell if the identification was genuine? It could have been a railway pass for all she knew. What *was* going on in her life? Nothing made sense anymore. She should have insisted on ringing Tim. She noticed the car was fitted with a mobile phone. She had never used one of those, but leant forward to the sergeant who sat in the front passenger seat.

"Could I use your phone to ring a friend?"

Without turning, he shook his close-cropped head. Jane sank back. She was so flustered she had not noticed where they were going. Now she could not tell where they were. She did not really know the countryside very well, in spite of the years she had lived there. The area just around Harvestdown, yes, but after that, well, after that it was an adventure needing a map.

After about half an hour they pulled into a long drive. They were still in the country, but Jane had noticed signposts to Worthing just a few miles away. They stopped in front of a Victorian mansion, the usual mixture of mock Tudor and turrets. It was now growing dark. Lights shone from many windows. They passed through a large porch and into an enormous hall, oak paneled with a wide staircase leading straight upwards.

Jane was taken through one of the several doors in the hall to a small sitting room, unexpectedly cozy with a chintz sofa and a large table on which were piled numerous magazines connected with country pursuits. Nevertheless, it did not feel lived in, more a waiting room. The sergeant told her to make herself comfortable. Jane sat nervously on the edge of the sofa, whilst he remained standing by the door. Constable North left the room and she heard his footsteps echoing across the hall.

Shortly, footsteps approached, lighter and quicker, female. A girl entered the room, tall, neat and precisely groomed but plain. She was wearing a crisp white blouse, blue skirt and blue pumps with low heels. No need for her to accentuate her height. She carried a tray of coffee and biscuits and set it on the table at Jane's elbow.

"Please help yourself."

The sergeant left the room and the girl took his place by the door. Jane's stomach was still churning and she had a bitter taste in her mouth. She was not sure that the coffee would help, but she poured herself a cup.

"How long do we have to wait?"

"Not long."

"What are we waiting for?"

There was no reply. The coffee was a mistake. The churning was turning to cramps.

"Is there a cloakroom?"

"Of course, follow me."

Jane followed the girl across the hall and down a short passage. The cloakroom had an outer lobby and an inner sanctum with a frosted glass door. Jane locked herself in but realised the girl was standing immediately outside. There was to be no privacy. Jane could not cope with that. She would have to manage with the discomfort. She counted to ten, flushed and unlocked the door. The girl, standing there, guessed and nodded a faint smile of apology. They returned to the sitting room. Jane ate a biscuit. Perhaps that would help settle things.

After about twenty minutes a buzzer rang. Once again they crossed the hall, went down a dark passage and descended a flight of stairs to a lower level. Ahead of them was a door covered in studded leather. Across the threshold, Jane found herself in a huge room, perhaps a games room or billiard room of the past. Like the hall, it was oak paneled. Heavy velvet curtains were pulled across windows at one end. There was a woven Indian carpet covering the centre, but the rest of the floor was highly polished parquet. The only furniture was a long wide table set across the room. In front of it was a single upright chair with arms. Behind sat three men. The only light in the room hung by a long flex to about eighteen inches above the table, and the heavy velour shade allowed light to escape downwards only. Thus the faces of the three men were invisible in the shadow.

A voice, apparently from the man in the middle, with a cultured but commanding ring, spoke.

"Miss Block, how good of you to come. We're sorry to have kept you waiting. Please sit down."

Jane sat. She gripped the arms of the chair tight; her knuckles shone white in the glow of the diffused light.

The man spoke again. "It appears an appropriate time for us to have a little chat."

Jane swallowed. "Are you part of the Special Branch thing?"

"Oh dear me, no. We're not police," the last word was uttered with disdain. "We are, let us say, guardians of the nation's integrity." He paused. "Of necessity we must remain anonymous to you. But in order that we can conduct our discussion this evening with manners, it will be in order to use our first names. You may call me Alistair, on my left is Henry, and on my right, Jeremy. You will forgive me if I call you Jane."

Jane said nothing. This was unbelievable.

"The matter we have to discuss with you is the manuscript of *The Hastings Option*."

Jane sat up. "How do you know about that?"

"Jane, knowledge is, how shall we say, our stock in trade."

Jane felt her fear ebbing and her temper rising. "I did not say *what* did you know, I said *how*."

"Ah, it is good to see that you have not lost your spirit. You will find the *what* interesting, but the *how* must remain confidential. Let us get on with the *what*. We know you have now acquired the manuscript of an account written by your late father of events which took place in the early stages of the war, when a number of distinguished persons, normally of a loyal and patriotic disposition, mistakenly concluded that the welfare of the country might best be achieved by following a course which in normal circumstances would be regarded as treason. Your late father was thought to be one of the plotters, although later claimed not to have been..."

"He wasn't," asserted Jane defensively.

"As you say. In any event, Lucian Feyrbaeme went on, as we know, to become a distinguished broadcaster and man of letters. But unknown to the public, he was pressing the authorities to take action against the misguided men, and some women, of that difficult period in the nation's history. He had trouble in accepting, it appears, that the overall interests of the nation would be best served by allowing matters to be forgotten."

"You mean a cover-up," Jane's temper was now near the boil.

"Crudely put, yes, but in the public interest."

"But these people were traitors!"

"They committed no treachery."

"But they did. They plotted to overthrow the government when the country was in peril. That is wicked treachery!"

"You take a narrow view."

"But you say you are the guardians of the nation's integrity. Does that include harbouring traitors?"

There was silence. Henry spoke. His voice was sinister, smooth and menacing.

"Did you know your mother was a Communist?"

"What?"

"A Communist agent. A minor one, certainly, but one you would call a traitor nevertheless. How does it feel to be the daughter of a traitor?"

"You're mad! You're all insane!"

Alistair spoke again. "I think you should listen to us, Jane. Your mother worked in the Foreign Office as a secretary. She associated with certain well-known defectors who caused great difficulties in the 1950's. They infected her with their misguided and traitorous sympathies. Because the authorities were anxious to limit the scale of the scandals and their own embarrassment, your mother escaped arrest."

There was a moment's silence. Jane gasped. Her thought process came to a full stop. She feared for a moment she was going to faint.

"I don't understand," she whispered.

Jeremy poured a glass of water from a carafe and slid it across the polished table towards her. Alistair continued.

"You have the right to offer your manuscript for publication. It is possible that the Government may feel it has the power to challenge that right in the courts. It would, however, be so much better for everyone if you yourself were to decide that no benefit will come from airing these events so many years after they happened, when knowledge of them could do no good."

Jane fought to regain control of her senses. "What are you asking?"

"That you deliver the manuscript to us. You may watch us destroy it."

In shock now, Jane became stubborn. "I won't do that. If I want to, I will publish."

Jeremy spoke. His voice was softer. There was the trace of an accent. Perhaps the West Country.

"There are risks, Jane."

"Risks?"

"This treachery, as you call it, permeated throughout the system of government. There are still a few survivors living, and of course, there are their families. Reputations would be at stake and much more besides. Even in the security services there are those who feel that sleeping dogs should be left to lie. Some of these elements are more aggressive in their attitudes than we are."

Jane stood up. "I will not be threatened. Thank you for telling me what you have. I should now like to go."

Alistair pushed a slip of paper towards her. A telephone number was written in pencil.

"Just call us here if you change your mind."

Jane took the paper and crumpled it into her pocket. "I think that most unlikely."

She heard a buzzer sound in the distance. Presumably they were calling the girl to escort her. The menacing voice of so-called Henry was speaking.

"I'm afraid we shall have to withdraw our protection."

"Protection? What do you mean?"

"Major Weldon."

"Major Weldon?"

"Major Timothy Gulliver Weldon."

Jane clung to the back of the chair for support.

"He was seconded to us from Army Intelligence, former SAS, one of their most cunning and skilful field officers."

The words seared through Jane's brain, *skilful, cunning*. The girl was at her elbow.

"This way please, Miss Block."

Jane turned without another word and followed her up the stairs towards the hall. She realised she was going to be sick. She turned and ran to the cloakroom. There was no time to close the door as Jane fell to her knees, heaving. The girl stood by and watched anxiously as Jane, head in the porcelain bowl and knees chilled by the cold tiles, endured the most wretched moments of her life.

CHAPTER FIFTEEN

The journey back to Harvestdown was a nightmare. Jane's life, so recently coming together, now lay in pieces. The girl sat beside her in the back of the car. She had spoken to the sergeant and constable, presumably to tell them that Jane was far from well, so the constable had stayed behind and the sergeant was driving. The girl had a woman's instinct for helping the needy and had given Jane a glass of water after her sickness. Jane wondered who she was. She was probably a member of the security services, or perhaps in the Special Branch. Jane glanced at her sideways. She did not look like a policewoman. Maybe she was another cunning field officer.

Jane, whose hand was in her coat pocket, felt her fingers close on the paper containing the number given to her by the three men. They passed through a village and the lights made it easy to read the number. Jane winced. It was the same number Tim had given her. The one she had rung leaving messages on his answering machine.

At last the car stopped outside the cottage.

"Would you like me to come in?" asked the girl.

"No thank you," said Jane.

"Are you sure you will be all right?"

Jane nodded. The car drove off as Jane fumbled for her key. Tim stepped forward from the shadows. Jane spun around.

"How dare you come here!"

"Jane, please, let me explain..."

"Explain what? How you are, what your superiors call, a cunning field officer? A brilliant operator who can cleverly trap unsuspecting females in distress into trusting you and believing all your lies?"

"Jane don't, it's not like that..."

"Oh yes it is. I can be fooled once, but not again. Just think, your job is just too good to be true. You make it up as you go along and all the time you are being paid by the taxpayer. I suppose it's all in a report. Did you tell them everything? What *did* flow from the pencil in your grubby little hand? Did you tell them what a clever seducer you were? Did you tell them you had a damn good fuck?!!" Jane was screaming now. She did not care if the neighbours heard. "Just think of it! Paid by the taxpayer for screwing! Do they give you free condoms as well?!"

Tim stepped forward and grabbed Jane by the shoulders and shook her.

"Jane! Pull yourself together! Listen..."

"Take your hands off me!" She beat his chest with her fists. "I hate you! I never want to see you again! Get out of my life! Go!"

Jane picked up the keys she had dropped to the ground and jabbed them into the locks. She stood in the doorway. He stood a few feet away, protesting.

Jane screamed again. "It was you who broke into Trubshaw's! That poor old man died of fright! You are vile. Evil. A murderer!"

Jane slammed the door and stood silently in the hall, her heart pounding in her chest, her head throbbing. Shortly she heard the bark and purr as Tim started the Jaguar. She listened to the scrunch of its wheels on the gravel of the drive as it pulled from the side of the house, followed by the squeal of rubber as it set off down the lane at speed.

Jane took her coat off and dropped it on the floor at her feet. Her happiness, her future, her sense of completeness, her fulfilment of life had vanished into the night. She walked silently into the sitting room, then fell onto the sofa. Soon, the little house echoed to the sobs of a shattered spirit and a broken heart.

Jane woke up to hear the telephone ringing. At first she did not know where she was. She was lying rumpled and fully clothed on the sofa. The clock on the chimney piece said nine fifteen. Her head ached and her mouth was bitter with bile. She struggled to the kitchen and lifted the receiver from the wall. Her voice was a hoarse whisper.

"Hello?"

The caller hesitated. "Jane, is that you?" It was Celia.

"Yes?"

"Darling, you sound ghastly."

"I had a bad night."

"Oh, poor you, but I know just how to cheer you up. Monty and I are off to Argentina tomorrow, but he is dying to meet you. He's at home today and we'd be thrilled if you could come over for lunch."

The thought of lunch almost made Jane gag. "Celia, I don't think I can manage it."

"Nonsense. I've woken you up, I can tell. In half an hour you will feel as right as rain. We'll make it a late lunch, continental style. We'll expect you between two and half past."

Jane could not think straight.

"Okay," she said, "see you then," and hung up. She could always call back a little later and cancel.

Jane sat down at the kitchen table and put her head in her hands. The mess in which she saw her life began to swim before her once again, but she had enough grip of herself to recognise the sinister nature of Celia's invitation. Why should Monty suddenly want to meet her? He knew perfectly well who she was. Those ridiculous men had spoken of aggressive elements from whom they claimed, preposterously, they were protecting her. Could Monty be part of this aggressive element? How could she believe those people anyway, after all the lies and deception of their cunning field officer? Perhaps it was all a smokescreen and they were the aggressive elements. Could it be that Monty wanted to help? He was, after all, married to her best friend, well, her only friend. Jane remembered she still had the clothes she had borrowed. She needed to return them.

All right then, she would pull herself together and go to the lunch. She would have to start getting her life together anyway and the quicker she started, the quicker she could get these frightful experiences behind her.

Jane went upstairs, had a bath, washed her hair and tried her best to patch up her wrecked face with her new cosmetic kit. Eventually, feeling surprisingly fresh and looking a lot better, she returned to the kitchen to make coffee and eat a bowl of flakes. It would do her good to have something inside her.

She concentrated her thoughts on Monty as a device for shutting out Tim. His grandfather had been a senior member of Churchill's government just below Cabinet level and might well have become the puppet Prime Minister. He was now dead, but Monty's father had only just retired as a respected MP, and Monty himself was an up-and-coming official in the Foreign Office. His mother, now a fully accepted member of the establishment, was an Argentine heiress. *Her* father, Monty's other grandfather, had not only been a successful businessman and industrialist known to the world, but in a former identity, a high ranking officer in the Waffen SS. Jane had no idea whether this former Nazi was still alive. He would be in his late eighties, probably, but even if he were dead, this family had a great deal to lose by the revelations in Lucian's manuscript.

As Jane drove off in her little car to keep her lunch engagement, she was in a determined mood. She had now lost confidence in her origins, in her connections and in her friends. It felt as if she were assailed on all sides by forces she could sense but not identify. Once again, she was on her own. But that was how she had lived before, and that is how she would survive from now on. Whatever the truth of this sorry affair, she would find it out. When she did, she would identify the guilty and make them pay.

The rumble of the car brought Celia through the open front door at the top of the steps. As ever, the welcome was gushing.

"Monty is on the terrace waiting for you, all agog. Darling, you've changed your hair. And make-up, too! You look stunning."

In spite of the compliments, Jane felt her confidence ebbing as she followed Celia, who floated ahead of her upon a wave of Chanel, billowy wisps of silk and golden hair. Monty stood on the terrace, back to the lawn, sunlight glinting in his cold blue eyes, hand outstretched in welcome.

"Jane. At last! I cannot forgive my jealous wife for keeping us apart for so long."

Under six-foot, his tanned face too puffy to be handsome, casual but sharp in an open-necked shirt and cotton slacks. He gripped Jane's hand, hesitantly offered and bent to kiss her on the cheek. Jane stood frozen.

"Let me give you a glass of champagne!"

"Just a little, because of the drive."

"Only the best. It will do you no harm."

Jane watched him pour from the black bottle of a Dom Perignon. How vulgar, she thought. They clinked glasses and sat together on well-cushioned wicker chairs. Jane felt as a fly hovering by the web of a spider. Monty spoke through moist lips in the soft, measured tones of a tormentor, sweetened by the drawl of an upper class English education and oiled by the flow of vast rivers of international money.

The conversation was trivial. Monty spoke of travel, alleging he had spent the last two months at the British Embassy in Lisbon promoting British business. What about Egypt, thought Jane. Celia did not want to be left out.

"Jane darling, where have you *been*? I've been trying to get you for weeks!"

"Oh," she said, "I had a trip to Egypt with an old friend to see the Pyramids and then," Jane found herself lying with unexpected skill, "a couple of weeks in the mountains of North Wales."

"Oh dear," said Celia sympathetically, "lots of rain. Frightful tourists in sandals and white cardigans. I went there once. But I can tell," she beamed at Jane, "by your tan that the sun shone for you!"

Monty cut in. "Scotland is best for mountains at this time of year. Fewer sandals too, if you go deep into the Highlands."

Jane laughed. A hollow, sociable laugh that did not come naturally to her. She hoped it sounded right and not as the cackle of a lunatic. Was Monty telling her he knew she was lying? She sipped her champagne nervously, seeking comfort from its gently rising bubbles.

Over lunch Monty spoke of politics. This seemed a device to silence his wife, who was entirely out of her depth. She made a brave attempt.

"I'm always bumping into politicians at all those receptions I have to go to with Monty. I can never tell one from another. They all look the same. Mind you, two nights ago a dear little man..."

"The Foreign Secretary," interjected Monty.

"No sweetie, he was English, not foreign," said Celia absently, "...patted my bottom and told me I was the most beautiful woman in the room. So at least some of them are human."

Jane chuckled. Monty looked cross. She decided to fish for information.

"Your father is a politician, isn't he, Monty?"

"He's retired now, but he was the Member for Polchester for over thirty years. Not much interested in government, mind you. A junior minister once or twice, but he preferred the freedom of the back benches."

"Unlike your grandfather?"

"Indeed yes. I think grandfather had ambitions to become Prime Minister, but things turned out differently after the war and the social tide was against him."

"Has your father given up politics for good?"

"Well, he hopes to become a life peer. My mother is absolutely determined to be Lady Polchester."

"Lady Polchester?"

"Dad has chosen his title already. He is hoping to be lucky in the New Year honours."

Jane feared that she was sounding like an inquisitor, but she pressed on. "Are you going to go into politics?"

"Interesting question. I want to get a little further in the Foreign Office, but perhaps after the next election I will resign. As Celia may have told you, my mother is from Argentina originally, and the family has substantial business interests in South America. The empire was founded by my Argentine grandfather. He is still alive, though very old. Upon his death, the control of the business passes to me. I cannot do that and remain in the civil service. Straight politics would then be easier."

So the Nazi grandfather was still alive. Jane was glad that she had been saved the question. Monty twisted the stem of his glass with chubby fingers.

"Celia tells me you are an artist."

"Commercial."

"You must let me see your work some time."

"My work?"

"We have so many business interests. We may be able to use you."

Jane finished her strawberries. Lunch had been chilled vichyssoise followed by poached salmon, all served by the maid, Theresa. They had continued with the Dom Perignon. Evidently there were plentiful supplies, but Jane had sipped sparingly. She wanted to keep her wits about her.

Afterwards, Monty took Jane's arm as they rose from the table. "Come, let me show you around the garden. We can join Celia on the terrace for coffee."

Celia took the hint. "I shall have to keep an eye on you, Jane, I think Monty has a soft spot for you already."

"Pay no attention," drawled Monty, gripping Jane's arm quite tightly, "just because Celia is always trawling for men, she assumes I do the same with women."

The exchange had a sharp edge. Jane wondered how long this marriage would last. In the garden Monty came to the point.

"I believe you have found the manuscript and I am sure you have read it. It will come as no surprise to you if I say that among our business interests we have a publishing house. On its behalf I should like to acquire the publishing rights."

"Publishing rights?"

"A euphemism. I want the manuscript. I will pay."

"How much?"

"Whatever you ask."

"Seven figures?"

"Without difficulty."

Jane's temptation was only momentary. "I shall not sell."

"Will you publish?"

"Yes," said Jane recklessly.

Monty smiled. "As you wish. Please remember that I tried to be fair and helpful."

Jane pursed her lips. Was he threatening her? Probably, but no matter. There was something she wanted to know.

"Monty, were you in Egypt?"

"Ah, so you recognised me. The answer is yes and, may I add, lucky for you that I was keeping an eye on you both."

"Why were you following us?"

"Well, that's interesting." Monty was reflective. "It was Weldon's theory that the manuscript was in Scotland. I fancied Lucian Feyrbaeme was more sophisticated. I thought his widow might be involved, especially as you rushed over to see her. When it transpired that you were both going to Egypt, it just occurred to me that it would be an ideal country in which to hide something from public view. I had some Foreign Office business which I could drum up. It was worth being sure."

Jane wanted to ask how he knew so much but she knew the answer. It was the trade of those grubby little men to know things. Helped by their cunning field officer. She regarded Monty with distaste. He returned her stare with a patronising grin. The terrace and Celia came into view.

Suddenly Jane felt pleased with herself. With his reference to Tim, Monty had given himself away. He *was* one of those grubby little men! Behind the table, with their faces in shadow. What cowards!

"We have no more to discuss," said Monty softly. "Let us enjoy our coffee."

Later, driving back to Harvestdown, Jane made further progress towards getting a grip of herself. She was relieved at the outcome of her conversation with Monty. She now knew what he was up to and where she stood with him. He had issued a mild threat, but Jane suspected that if she did decide to publish, his first reaction would be to raise his offer and then to fight it in the courts. Other families mentioned in the manuscript had almost as much to lose, but with Monty, the Nazi grandfather and his still ambitious mother would add an extra dimension.

By the time Jane reached home, she had formulated a plan. She would go away for the weekend and stay in a hotel, accessible to Cambridge for Mitzi's funeral the following Tuesday, but not in Cambridge itself. Perhaps on the Norfolk coast. There she would rest and think. After the funeral, she would drive back to Scotland. Jane would ask Mr Linnett to obtain the manuscript and she would take it with her. She would study it carefully and make her decision about publication in Skye.

Up there she would go through the house carefully. There were bound to be clues and mementoes from her parents' life. There may even be a direct communication to her from Lucian. A letter or diary or some such. She would be in no hurry. A month perhaps, after which she would return to the south and pursue whatever course she had decided upon.

As Jane locked up the garage, ears singing from the noise of the engine, she made up her mind on another adventurous step. She would buy a new car. The 2CV had been ideal for shopping and the short journeys she had made within the narrow confines of her simple life before, but now she needed something suitable for long distance travel. She would ring the bank manager in the morning and arrange for him to sell sufficient securities to clear whatever cheque she paid out when she had made her choice. After that, she would spend the day organising her new transport. There was no doubt about it, once you re-established a sense of purpose, life began to look up.

By lunchtime the next day she had made her choice. She found just the very thing at a garage in Chichester. The salesman was older than such people usually were and Jane trusted him. It was a Ford Escort Cabriolet with fuel injection. Demonstration model, apparently, with only three thousand recorded miles. It looked and smelled completely new. Its performance seemed to Jane to be in the Ferrari class and she received an excellent price for the 2CV. The man promised to have the car ready by three o'clock, so she gave him her cheque in order that he could telephone the bank and confirm that it would be met.

Jane then set off into the town to one of the chain stores and bought herself a silk headscarf and a pair of dark glasses. Both designer items and very expensive. She then went to a music shop and bought some tapes, as the new car had a stereo system. The 2CV had only a radio, and that was difficult to hear. The excitement brought on an appetite. On the spur of the moment she decided on a burger. Normally she would not even consider junk food, but today she found herself ordering a hamburger with chips, washed down by cola.

Afterwards she felt a little uncomfortable from the unaccustomed bulk of the meal and the gassy drink, but she decided that was a price well worth paying for the enjoyment. She kept reminding herself of the importance of fresh vegetables, but decided that just for today, ketchup was much more fun.

At about the time Jane was choosing her car, Monty and Celia were completing the checking-in process at Heathrow Airport. Before moving into the departure lounge, Monty looked at his watch, a magnificent, handmade chronograph by Baume et Mercier, which told him that it was exactly midday. He excused himself from his wife and went to the lavatory. There he stood facing the tiled wall with others, some of them travellers, some of them seeing off or meeting friends, who sought relief from nature's demands in what Americans euphemistically call a restroom. Like the others, he took shallow breaths to avoid inhaling the acrid air. No one spoke, concentrating on the matter that had brought them here and the flight announcements broadcast with a clarity unmatched anywhere else in the airport.

Monty took a place at the end of the line. Beside him on his left stood a shortish man, rather plump, wearing a dark blue felt hat and a dark blue pinstripe. With infinite care and with hardly a perceptible movement, certainly not one which would be noticed by others, he slipped a large brown envelope, quite thick and evidently full of papers, from beneath his right arm and under Monty's left. Gripping the package carefully against his side, Monty withdrew to the washbasin. After rinsing his hands he walked quietly out of the premises, stuffing the packet in his flight bag as he did so.

A few moments later, the short, plump man in the dark blue suit followed to the washbasin, where he remained washing his hands thoroughly with soap and water, after which he dried them at a noisy electric blower. By the time he left the lavatory Monty and Celia had passed through into the departure lounge. The man made his way towards the car park. A man of no significance whom nobody noticed, but had Jane been at the airport that day instead of buying a car in Chichester, she would have recognised Mr Linnett immediately.

CHAPTER SIXTEEN

After studying maps and consulting a handbook listing guesthouses and hotels, Jane settled on Ipswich, or rather, a village just outside the city where there was a country house hotel with up to date leisure facilities including an indoor swimming pool. The location would give easy access to the coast as well as to Cambridge. After the funeral she would drive straight on to Scotland, spending the night somewhere en route.

Once again, Jane went through the process of closing up the house. She packed her belongings into the capacious boot of her new car, feeling much more confident about her journey and not a little stylish. The day was bright and warm, enabling her to put the hood down, show off her silk scarf and designer shades. She had even painted her nails. Not too red, just a soft pink to match her cotton shirt, which she had combined with her jeans and leather moccasins. Her bare ankles and arms still sported the Egyptian tan, which had faded remarkably little. When she pulled off to the motorway service station to fill up with petrol, she was conscious of admiring glances from beer-bellied salesmen in their white shirts and dark grey trousers, worn shiny by days spent in endless driving.

The hotel proved an ideal choice. Just the place for her to rest, heal and reflect. She spent the few days swimming, eating, exploring Ipswich, its harbour and the coast, and sitting lazily on the terrace in the bright sunshine sipping afternoon tea, or, in the early evening before dinner, margaritas in memory of Mitzi.

Jane paid little attention to the other guests, couples mostly, and generally elderly. She made no attempt to strike up conversations. They, detecting her solitary inclination, left her alone. This suited Jane perfectly, because she wanted to think. Above all, she wanted to think about herself. What were her beginnings? Why had Lucian deserted or at least detached from his pregnant lover? Where did Robert Block come into this triangle? How much could she believe of what those awful men had said?

She considered her mother. It would, of course, make sense. Diana Block had always had a bitter, fatalistic streak. She had smoked and drunk without caution or conscience, as if her life was without value. Within her limitations she looked after Jane quite well, but without the insurance money and the boarding school education, Jane's life would have been grim. She could now see that her mother would not have been able to cope. Yet why had Diana been a Communist? She was not an intellectual, and although her background was more or less working class, it was very respectable. It was certainly not revolutionary.

Was Lucian communist? He was strongly anti-fascist, and by all accounts his television inquisitions of politicians, particularly those of the centre and the right were pretty ruthless. Before his writing and broadcasting career, Lucian had been at the Home Office during the early Cold War period when Communism, though not illegal, was certainly taboo. Clearly there must have been something that drew Diana and Lucian together, because from all Jane had so far discovered, they were very different people.

Of course, Jane did not know for sure that this communist business was a reality. It would not surprise her if those dreadful men had made it all up to disorientate her. Nevertheless Jane suspected that it was true. She had always thought there was something strange about her mother. A tragic figure hiding a secret.

Jane tried not to think about Tim, yet when her defences had been broken down by margaritas or wine, she could not help herself. She hated him for his deceptions. She despised him for the job he did, but in spite of everything, the days with Tim had been the happiest of her life.

There was a curious extra mystery now. If Tim was not Paul Harvey, who was? Or was that part of his life true? Was he an intelligence officer and a writer? Why had he chosen that author, whose books actually existed, as a cover if it was not Tim himself?

That reminded her. She rang Mr Linnett and asked him to bring the manuscript to the funeral. He hesitated a moment.

"Are you sure it will be safe?"

"As sure as I am of anything at the moment," responded Jane with some resignation.

"Very well, as you wish."

As Jane put down the phone she thought that Mr Linnett sounded rather put out.

On the other side of the world, a limousine, its interior cooled by air-conditioning, bounced along dusty roads, as potholes, those which the chauffeur could not avoid, tested the suspension of the car. After such a long flight, this part of the journey seemed longer than it actually was. A helicopter would have been easier, but there was a risk that it would attract attention, so they always travelled by road. Celia, oblivious to events of which she was a part, dozed with her head on Monty's shoulder. The packet, the contents of which Monty had now read, was back in the flight bag that rested beneath his protecting hand on the bouncing seat beside him. At last, the gateway to the ranch came in to view. The car moved smoothly now up the avenue of trees to the sprawling Spanish style mansion.

Monty left his wife to make her own way to their suite for a shower and change, whilst he followed a corridor to a second marble staircase which led to the old man's quarters. He found him sitting in his wheelchair on the balcony, a small flask containing schnapps and a jug of iced water on a small table within easy reach. As his grandson approached, he looked up with identical cold blue eyes, though sunken now with age. Monty set the packet in his lap. His brown speckled hand, thin and claw-like, pulled the papers from the envelope. When he saw the title page he gave a long, slow sigh. His crooked fingers smoothed the pages, whilst he lifted his gaze toward Monty and smiled. His grandson looked at the thin white hair and the wrinkled features burnished dark by the years of the Argentine sun, wondering at the secrets of fearful deeds which lurked deep in the memory behind the fading eyes.

When Tuesday came in East Anglia, the day was overcast, the bright spell was over. The weather was solemn, like the antiseptic interior of the crematorium chapel. Unlike a church, which celebrated christenings, weddings and other joyful occasions, these places specialised in grief only. A production line of sorrow, shunting mortal remains through fire into ashes, whilst the red-eyed mourners sniffed and pondered the question of immortality.

Jane was clad in a grey dress, short black jacket and black hat, a little heavy for the summer even on a gloomy day, but the leftovers from her mother's funeral. There was no point in buying new. She rather fancied that Mitzi would prefer bright colours, but the old lady had apparently left no instructions. Mr Linnett had put an announcement in the death columns of national broadsheets, giving brief particulars of the deceased, but declaring the funeral private with no flowers, please. Hardly surprising, therefore, that apart from Mitzi, Mr Linnett and the undertakers, there was no one else there. She had rather hoped that Tim would relent and appear, shame-faced, to plead, but there was no sign of him.

The brief service was conducted by a clergyman who was a complete stranger to everyone. Jane wiped tears from her eyes and blew her nose. She was, she reflected, the only person there who was not being paid to be present, but her emotion was shed not so much for the death of her friend, whose passing she had now accepted, as for the absence of her lover whose estrangement had left a sickening void in her heart.

Afterwards, Mr Linnett handed Jane the envelope containing the manuscript and suggested lunch at a local hotel. Jane declined this courtesy, though she did speak briefly to him about her inheritance. Most of it was the main part of Lucian's estate, left on his death to Mitzi. He seemed to have invested quite a bit, and the shares had grown in value over the years. There were also a few royalties from Lucian's many works, some of which were still in print.

She made exhilarating progress on her journey north in spite of the traffic, stopping on the A1 for a bowl of soup and a granary roll. She stayed for the night at a bed and breakfast in Penrith, where the cheerful red-faced landlady provided a clean bed and a wholesome dinner at a very reasonable price.

It was mid-afternoon the following day that Jane first caught sight, through murky weather, of Loch Alsh, but by the time she reached the ferry, a patch of sun had broken through. As she watched its effect on the rippling water and the hills of the island beyond, she treated it as a sign of welcome, and in a curious way, felt that she was coming home.

Later on, as she rummaged through the croft and found bedding and blankets spotless and aired and ready for use, and basic provisions in the larder put there by Mrs MacFee. She felt cosy and safe. She would enjoy the coming weeks of self-discovery, after which she hoped looming decisions would take care of themselves.

CHAPTER SEVENTEEN

Over the following weeks Jane began the intoxicating process of discovering her heritage and, through it, to make better sense of her tangled past. She had expected there might be some sort of note from Lucian explaining that he was her father and why it was they had never met. But although she had a strong sense of his presence, and her mother's too, as she searched through the house, there was no direct message. In many ways Jane was relieved at this. She might have found his explanation disappointing, and it would have hung heavily with her to the end of her days.

As it was, she could make her own opinion from what she saw and read and found. Maybe that is how he intended it, but then again he had died prematurely. He must have expected to live for years, so he probably thought there was plenty of time. She realised that she was looking at the way he lived here. When he had last closed the door on the little property, he had expected to return. It must have been Trubshaw, who at some time had brought the deeds and the manuscript and set them in the bureau, or maybe he sent them to McAllister.

She was hoping to meet McAllister, but according to Mrs MacFee, he was away in Aberdeenshire fishing for a month. His annual holiday, apparently. Annoyingly, he had set off the day before she arrived. So questions concerning Trubshaw, who was the person who had known Lucian best, would have to wait until he returned. It might even be that McAllister had met Lucian, so she may be able to look forward to a first hand account.

Jane started with the deeds. These indicated that the property had been acquired by Lucian in 1948 for a tiny sum and transferred into Jane's own name in 1952, the year of her birth. This meant her mother would have joined Lucian for those long summer breaks for four years before the two parted when Jane was born. They may have been visiting earlier and staying in guesthouses or rented accommodation until they bought the croft. There would have been comparatively few visitors in those days. The island was hardly crowded now.

Next Jane turned her attention to the books. There were a surprising number of these in a fitted bookshelf that covered a complete end wall of the living room. Jane concluded that this was very much the library of an academic on holiday. It was almost all classics, poetry and literature. Many of the great names were there, Byron, Tennyson, Keats, Wordsworth, Trollope, Jane Austen, Tolstoy and Ibsen. There were lighter works,

Dickens and Conan Doyle, and a few detective stories by the popular female authors of the 1930's. Jane suspected that these were for her mother.

There were books, too, on mountaineering, the hills and mountains of Scotland and one that concentrated on climbing in Skye. Within the pages of this she found little annotations and dates showing when Lucian and Diana had completed the walks or climbed the peaks. Lucian's own books were there, too. Jane did not think these were to her taste. There were his earlier biographies of Victorian adventurers, Jane had never heard of any of them, and two later works published in the 1960's. One was about contemporary politics of the day. As the politics concerned were no longer contemporary, it looked heavy going. Another was about subordinate generals of the Second World War, not the great well-known commanders, but the divisional commanders, major generals, who had played critical roles in the various battles but were little recognised outside military circles. All nationalities were included: British, French, Italian, American, German, Russian, Japanese and Australian. For students of military history the volume might have been interesting, but Jane hated war and understood nothing of martial arts.

She was about to set the book on one side when, on impulse, she began to thumb through the pages and look at the photographs. Suddenly there was a face that she instantly recognised. The caption described Major General Gordon Gulliver Weldon. There was no mistaking the likeness, though of course, a different generation. This must be Tim's father. The text told how this daring commander of an armoured division in Horrocks's Corps under Montgomery had spearheaded many an attack in the great slog from Normandy to Luneberg Heath in Germany, where the war on the western front had finally ended. Lucian must have at least interviewed this man, or may even have been friends with him. He probably met the young Tim. Tim was a shade older than Jane, but would have been born well after the war. Maybe the General married later in life. Anyway, there had been a connection that Jane previously had not suspected.

Tim clearly knew more about Lucian than he had been willing to say. Jane fancied he probably was Paul Harvey after all. There must be plenty of time in the long spying hours to dream up plots, but why had he not said anything? What was he trying to hide? Why always lies? Why could he never speak the truth? The only way for Jane to find the answers to these questions was to confront him, but she was not ready for that yet. Tim was out of her life, and for the moment, that is how he would have to stay.

It was in the bottom drawer of the bureau that Jane found the photo albums, and when she opened these, she found to her delight a record of her parents' life together, full of happiness and carefree days. Snapshots began in 1947, so they must have spent an earlier year before buying the property. There were black and white pictures of picnics, walks, bathing on deserted beaches and climbing in the mountains. The pictures were remarkably clear. One of them must certainly have possessed a camera of high quality. Jane guessed it would be Lucian. She could not recall her mother taking much interest in photography. The camera was fitted with a self-timing device, because many of the pictures were of the two of them a little askew, suggesting it was resting on a sloping surface. This explained the antler photo which had led her here. She was a touch disappointed. She had somehow hoped that the image had been taken by Robert, rather than by the camera's own handiwork, but of him there was no sign or reference of any kind. However her Daddy fitted into the relationship, it was clear he had no connection with Skye.

There was a casual, informal atmosphere. This was well before the days of fleece mountain jackets and stretch trousers. Old tweeds and baggy sweaters with, in Mitzi's words, hobnailed boots, formed the trekking kit of those times, and much more sensible, too, thought Jane. All this hi-tech clothing was a ridiculous waste of money unless you were going up Everest. They appeared to have a little car, an open Morris 8, pre-war. Later this was replaced by a Morris Minor, once again with a hood. The pictures of the roads showed these often little better than tracks. Although today many were still narrow, wide enough for only one car at a time with passing places, they were well maintained and had good smooth surfaces.

There was a wonderful nostalgic air to all this. It gave the impression that life was simpler and with fewer worries. Probably this was not the case. There was food rationing in those days, the Cold War cast a chill shadow, young men had to undergo a period of compulsory military service and there were so called *flash points* all over the world. So the sense of freedom which Jane caught from the pages of little black and white pictures was probably an illusion, but one which Lucian and Diana must have been at pains to create on their annual escape.

When Jane had finished looking through all the albums she wondered whether Lucian and Diana had been in love. Either way it left the unanswered question. Why on earth had Diana and Lucian split up and her mother married Robert when she was pregnant? Had there been a row? Somehow Jane did not sense this. Everything was too happy and carefree.

Mind you, if there had been, Lucian would have had plenty of time to erase the signals from the cottage before he died. But then he would not have left the place to Diana in the first instance. He would have left it straight to Jane. Or neither.

It was very emotional going through what was now her home, yet was also a living museum of the life Lucian and Diana had led there. Although fifteen years had passed between the ending of their summer visits and Lucian's death, Jane fancied that Lucian had not visited often during this period. There were no snapshots or self-portraits. Mitzi had said that Lucian went to Cornwall fishing after the liaison with Diana ended. Jane began to suspect that he had left the property almost entirely unchanged in order to preserve a relic of his secret life with her mother. This must have been why he built the bungalow next door for the MacFees, so that nothing would be spoiled or altered. It was only recently that Harold Trubshaw had modernised the heating and cooking arrangements, probably in anticipation of Jane wanting to spend time here and needing more modern facilities than those which were acceptable in the immediate post-war era.

Mostly during the day, whenever it was fine, Jane spent the time out of doors. She drove to all parts of the island, becoming familiar with its geography, and using the old guides from the bookshelf, visited all the places of interest which must have been frequented by her parents. She walked on deserted beaches and climbed in the foothills, avoiding the peaks but achieving what Tim had called the outriders and, in the Black Cuillins, the corries. These were the high semi-circular plateaux at the base of the ascents to the main ridge.

She grew accustomed to her surroundings and her heritage. Her wounded soul began to heal. She came to terms with the twists and turns that her life had taken, the hopes and disappointments, and with a pragmatic stoicism which was very much part of her character, took stock of her life and decided that she had a lot to be thankful for. She had her career as an illustrator, which she must return to in the autumn, she had her home in Sussex, and now this retreat far into this wonderful island off the west coast of Scotland, out of reach of all who were not enthusiasts for its rugged grandeur.

Although there were still mysteries, instinctively she felt the story was not all bad. She had made new friends and lost them. Mitzi through death, Tim through deceit and desertion, but in a short period each had brought a new dimension to her life. Mitzi had opened her eyes to the world and Tim had opened her eyes to her body. Before, she had thought of herself as getting old. Now she felt she was quite young. There could be other relationships and the world was waiting for her to explore it. There had been compensations, too. The inheritances gave her complete financial independence and her earnings from her career would provide the resources for travel. The only sordid element was the manuscript and the shadowy figures who were taking so much interest in it.

Jane had deliberately not read it again. She wanted to reach her decision first. She was thankful that Mr Bremmer was willing to offer so much money, guaranteeing that she would not in a moment of weakness sell to the dreadful Monty. Yet she wondered if the public really would be interested in these revelations, which would be hotly disputed by historians, of events surrounding a generation of which only an elderly remnant now survived. The media, of course, would love it. There would be endless articles and commentaries, serialisation, probably, in one of the Sunday papers. Jane herself would become a focus of publicity, interviews on the radio, television, even. Did she want that? Did she want the money?

The money question was easy to answer. It would make her feel uncomfortable to acquire money by such a means. Publicity would attach to this aspect and she might be accused of publishing for gain, when in reality, if she published it would be for conscience. Would anybody take that seriously? She thought not. In the end, modern society was too materialistic and avaricious ever to believe that she, Jane Block, was not like that. Then there was the question of the modern generation of the families involved. Should they walk under a cloud because of what their fathers and grandfathers did? Was that fair? If this business about her mother being a communist was true, might not she herself be attacked for being the offspring of treachery? Mind you, those awful men had not said her mother passed secrets to potential enemies, only that she was either a member of, or sympathiser with, a reviled party. Nevertheless there were plenty of opportunities for media exploitation of Jane's own background.

In the end, Jane had almost reached the decision to destroy the manuscript and let the secrets remain secrets forever, when something happened to change her mind. Looking through the bookshelf late one evening for something to read before going to sleep, she came upon a small volume right at one end of the lower shelf, which she had previously missed. It was *The Diary of Anne Frank*. Of course she had heard of this, but she had never seen the film nor read the book. That night she started to read. She read late and all through the next day when a storm blew and rain beat upon the panes.

Jane was deeply moved by the tragic simplicity with which this doomed and innocent girl had recorded her hopes and sufferings before finally being taken by the centurions of one of the most perverted racial doctrines in history. Towards the end of the day, the storm abated, the sun came out and Jane finished reading.

She stood in the porch beneath the antlers, a tiny scrap of domestic architecture unchanged from the image on the crumpled snapshot which had brought her here, and watched the white clouds scurrying fast and high across the sky. Jane remembered the part of the armistice terms which the traitors were willing to sign, which would have enabled the Gestapo and the SS to round up all the German Jews and German nationals so as to ship these tragic and innocent people to suffering and death in the camps and ovens. Perhaps there had been more terrible crimes in history, but Jane knew of none, and now she felt that anyone who had condoned or had sympathy with these monstrous aims should suffer the consequences.

She would publish. She would not take the money. She would arrange with Mr Bremmer for it to be sent to charities that specialised in helping refugees and people who suffered from racial conflict wherever it may happen. She would give no interviews and allow no personal publicity. That would be handled by her publishers or her solicitor. Mr Linnett should be well able to cope. She thought of Mitzi's parents. They, too, would have been dragged off, as would Mitzi herself! Monty and his family would have to answer for their connections. Let the new Lady Polchester apologise for her father hiding away in South America, as his life slowly ebbed its wicked way. Let them explain at their cocktail parties and receptions on what grisly and cursed foundation their fortune had grown.

Yes, that is what Jane would do.

Next day, after waking to beautiful sunshine, Jane spent the morning on the shore of the loch watching the seales. Later she made a light lunch, and now feeling ready for the task ahead she brought a chair into the little porch and settled herself with the big brown envelope. Now that she had made up her mind, she would re-read *The Hastings Option* with a comprehending and purposeful mind. She slit the top of the envelope with her nail and tipped the manuscript out on her lap.

Jane stared at the sheaf of papers in disbelief. They were blank sheets. There was not a vestige of type on any of them. The manuscript had gone.

CHAPTER EIGHTEEN

All afternoon and into the evening Jane sat in the porch. At first she tried to think of some rational explanation. A mistake by Mr Linnett? A mistake by the Bank in whose vaults it had been put for safe keeping? Slowly the awful reality dawned. The manuscript been stolen. But how? When? By whom? It was complete when she handed it to Mr Linnett. Was it complete when he returned it? Had someone broken in up here?

Quite suddenly Jane did not care. Not just about the manuscript, but about anything. Over these past weeks she had seen a cocoon of predictable security and isolation melt in the heat of a life of challenge and opportunity. She had discovered feelings, friendship, love, adventure and true happiness. But unlike her cocoon, which had protected her unchanging for so long, these new spices of life had overwhelmed, like exotic aromas caught in the steam of an oriental kitchen, to be lost when the cooking was over and the fire was out. With dismay Jane saw that the cocoon, too, was gone. Formed largely out of ignorance or, rather, of a fear of knowledge, it could not be restored. Yes she had experiences of people, emotions and events, but these were complicated by riddles and uncertainties, betrayals and threats.

Only yesterday she felt buoyant. A buoyancy stemming from her rationalisation about the discoveries of her origins and a feeling that she was once again in control of her own destiny. On her own, after much soul searching, she had made a decision to publish *The Hastings Option*. No one had persuaded her. She had made up her own mind. Her decision would, for the first time, impact not only upon her own life but on the lives of others. It would challenge her own endurance, pillory the guilty, spare the innocent and honour those sacrificed in that dark moment of history. But above all it would restore her confidence in herself. Self worth had never before been a quality Jane had enjoyed in any measure, but she was on the brink of achieving it. Now that fulfilment was taken from her. She had been outwitted. Cast aside. Ridiculed. Quite suddenly, she felt hollow. Broken. Yes, that's how she felt. Broken.

Yet why broken? What had been lost? Just some dubious history that no longer mattered, surely? But that was the point. It did matter. Jane had been given the responsibility to make sure that it mattered. The honour of her country was compromised. The sacrifices of the people of these islands, given in defence of the civilised values upon which that honour was based, were insulted by the fact of these traitors and their families living untainted, under the very freedoms they had been willing to throw away. Fate had chosen that Jane was the one who would bring all this to the light of the modern day. And what had happened? She had failed. This was not a responsibility for herself. Just for once, it was for others. For others, and she had let them down.

Without thinking, Jane took her coat from behind the door and began to walk over the peat towards the cliff. The ground, as always, was damp and her shoes were not really up to it and soon began to leak. Absently she realised she should have worn her boots, but it was of no consequence. Nothing was of any consequence anymore. She no longer wanted to know why Lucian was her father, why her mother married Robert, if and why she was a Communist, why Tim befriended her only to betray her, why she had at last fallen in love, but with such a bitter outcome.

The sun was setting as she reached the cliffs. The day had been bright with few clouds, but these were now gone. The horizon was clear, bathed orange in the glow of the sunset. Gulls swooped below her, mostly in silence now at the close of the day, skimming down to a docile sea, maybe for fun or maybe for a last snack before night. Jane reflected how easily the solitary calm could become a drenching, buffeting, angry scene, as Atlantic storms rode landward upon their isobars to batter the peaks and scream through the glens. But this evening all was serene.

Jane caught the mood and in her anguish, she too, became calm. No longer was she troubled by what she should know or do, nor by what might have been. Just as the sun was sinking with the ebbing day, Jane began to ebb from herself, to disconnect, to float as an onlooker of her own persona, no more a part of her body than of the gulls, or cliffs, or the soft breeze, rising salt tipped from the waves below. It would be so easy to walk that body forward three paces and watch it fall, bouncing in slow motion from crag to crag until it plunged, lifeless, beneath the sea, its past too muddled to cope with the present or face the future.

Jane closed her eyes and saw her life unravel like a rewinding video, each frame vivid in its moment of exposure, yet lost in a fraction of a second. There was Tim, Mitzi, Celia, her mother, the man she called Daddy, the love, the hope, the fear, the joy, the gloom. Above all there was the emptiness of her life alone. It was an empty existence, empty of purpose and contribution. Nothing would be different if she stepped forward. Nobody would miss her, no great project would go unfulfilled, no group would go hungry, no heads would bow in mourning. Perhaps

Celia would shed a tear, but only in passing between one vacuous thought and another. Surely better to float out towards the gilded sun to be forever a part of the waves, the cliffs and the soaring gulls?

Behind her Jane caught the sound of a footfall on the peat. She did not turn.

So, had they come to finish her?

Those silly men to throw her over?

Well she was ready. She took a deep breath and waited as the rhythmic sound approached ever closer. With her eyes still tight shut, Jane braced her legs so that she might use the push she was sure was coming to leap into the void, one thousand feet above the ocean.

Almost upon her, the footsteps halted. A strong hand gripped her arm and pulled her gently back. A man's voice, old but firm, spoke with a hint of Scottish brogue.

"I would not stand too close. The gulls may glide, but you would drop like a stone."

The spell was broken. Jane opened her eyes and turned towards a scent of tobacco and warm tweed, to face a man, full bearded, with twinkling grey eyes and silver hair flowing beneath a deerstalker hat. He wore a long coat almost to his ankles.

"Jock McAllister. You will be Jane Block, I think. I called at the croft but you had already set out on your walk. You will forgive me for following, but these cliffs are dangerous to the unwary, especially in the fading light."

He held out his hand. Its warmth caught the chill of Jane's own, proffered nervously in response. She could not find her voice. McAllister peered at her, waiting.

Shortly, sensing that there had been some sort of emotional crisis, he spoke again.

"Come now, it's best we return to your croft. The sunset is a beguiling display, but with clear skies and autumn near, the temperature falls sharply once it has sunk."

Purposefully he took Jane's arm. From within the huge coat he produced a long flashlight of the kind used by security guards. The powerful beam set their course back towards the cottage. McAllister's grip on Jane's arm was tight. At last she managed to speak.

"You must forgive me. I was in a sort of daydream. I really am pleased to see you, Mr McAllister."

He turned towards her. In the half-light Jane could no longer make out his features, but she sensed that twinkling eye.

"None of this "mister" business." For a second he hesitated. "Call me Jock."

Jane nodded. "Of course Jock! It's just that Mrs MacFee always calls you Mr McAllister. That's how I think of you." Jane managed a shy smile which he did not see.

They walked on in silence. Jane was too drained to think of anything to say and McAllister, having broken the ice, was keeping his counsel. At length they reached the cottage. Jane turned on the light in the kitchen. McAllister followed her in.

"What you need right now," he said, as he hung his coat behind the door to reveal tweed breeches and a Hebridean sweater, "what you need is a strong cup of sweet tea." With that he turned and filled the kettle.

Sensing Jane's surprise he ventured, "I have been managing this place to have it ready for you, so I know my way around the basics."

Jane smiled again, this time with more confidence, and sat down at the table. Soon she was sipping the steaming mug McAllister put in front after. It was certainly strong. There was plenty of sugar too, but it was not unpleasant.

"Jock, what about you? Would you prefer coffee or something?"

He shook his head. "Not just now, but if you could cope I would light a pipe."

Jane was not too sure about this. She would never allow anyone to smoke at The Hollies after her mother died. Not that anyone came there anyway. She quite liked the smell of pipe tobacco, which nowadays one seldom encountered. Just here in the kitchen would be all right surely? The pipe seemed so much a part of the beard and the tweeds.

She smiled once more. "Of course. I think I might enjoy the aroma." She added, "I think Lucian was a pipe smoker. I found some old ones in a box."

McAllister's grey eyes looked at Jane quizzically. "I forget," he said.

There was another silence as Jane watched the careful filling, from a leather pouch, of a large curved briar, well smoked. There followed a huge combustion as McAllister used an old Zippo lighter at the edge of the bowl. He stood by the stove puffing thoughtfully, as Jane inhaled the aroma of an expensive, handcrafted blend.

Suddenly inquisitive, she asked, "What do you do, Jock, apart from keeping an eye on this place?"

He stopped puffing and took the pipe from his mouth.

"I am a writer."

God! Another one, thought Jane. "Do you write under your own name?"

"No. My pen name is Paul Harvey."

Jane's heart missed a beat.

"Did you say Paul Harvey?"

McAllister nodded.

"Inspector Garlick?"

McAllister nodded again.

"But, I thought…" Jane stopped. She did not know how to explain Tim and his claim to be the elderly author now before her.

McAllister walked over to the table and laid his pipe, now out, upon the scrubbed surface. His eyes regarded Jane intently as he spoke again.

"That is not quite all I'm afraid. There is no easy way to say this."

He hesitated. Jane's heart was pounding. In spite of the tea her mouth had become bone-dry.

"My real name is Lucian Feyrbaeme. I believe, Jane, you are my daughter."

CHAPTER NINETEEN

At first Jane could not focus on the words she had just heard. Subconsciously she understood exactly what they meant, but her conscious mind had gone blank. It had, in computer jargon, crashed. The two stared at each other, neither moving. Lucian standing at the end of the table, Jane seated halfway along on his left. Slowly she began to shake, then to heave almost convulsively. A wild and unfamiliar sound echoed in the kitchen, pitched between a groan and a scream. It fought its way through Jane's clenched teeth, coming, it seemed, not from her throat nor even from deeper in her body. It was, felt Jane, who was now only dimly aware of the echo around her, a cry from her very soul. She saw Lucian approach her, doubtless to offer some comfort, but in her confusion she thought he might strike her and threw up her hands to defend herself, recoiling back into her chair as she did so. This surge of fear had a curious effect, as almost at once Jane could feel her self-control returning.

She fell silent as Lucian disappeared into the sitting room. She heard him rummaging in the corner cupboard. Soon he returned with a bottle of local whisky and two tot-sized tumblers. Jane rose unsteadily from her chair and stood by the window, her face deathly pale against the backdrop of the darkness beyond the panes. She spoke, her voice weak, as he stood in the doorway.

"I'm sorry about that. I lost myself. It is becoming a habit."

Jane knew she had suffered some kind of emotional event. She could recall everything as it happened, from the moment she found the manuscript was missing, to this instant now. But there was an odd sensation that she had observed rather than lived through her experiences. She had heard of nervous breakdowns but they supposedly lasted months. It was as if she had left the rails of self-awareness, like some runaway train, but was now back on the track. Such a violent sequence of mood swings was outside her experience. She hoped it was never to be repeated. Her confidence trickled back.

There in front of her was the answer to all the riddles and mysteries of her life and her origins, looking awkward clutching a bottle and two small tumblers. How should she react to this phoenix, just arisen from the ashes of the past? To welcome? To reject? To admonish?

She took a deep breath, sighed, then sat down at the table again, drained of her scarce energy. She felt her recovery from her emotional wobble would be helped if she could have a really good cry. But she must get a grip and retain control of her wits.

Lucian pushed a tot of whisky forward. About to refuse, Jane changed her mind. She was not sure whether this was out of bravado, defiance or desperation, but she swallowed it in one go. It was as if she had swallowed molten lava. She fought the reflex to choke. Lucian spoke.

"It has quite a kick. Matured in wood over ten years at least. It will steady you and make what I have to say less offensive."

Jane was not convinced. This extraordinary, yet homely, old man had a lot to explain. Would he come clean or would there be more lies? Would she be able to tell?

Lucian paused to produce the Zippo. Jane was surprised to find the aromatic pipe smoke soothing, as it wreathed itself around his head, drifting upwards to hang beneath the low kitchen ceiling. When Lucian began it was early evening. When he finished it was early morning. At first they stayed in the kitchen as Jane listened to Lucian in the chill silence of reproach. Later, after a break for scrambled eggs around midnight, by which time Jane's perspective had become a little less judgemental, they settled in the sitting room to continue her extraordinary voyage of self discovery. She suspected it was, to Lucian, a release of a great burden, long carried in hope that it might one day be shed. Finally at four thirty she went up to bed, whilst Lucian lay down to sleep on the sofa. When they parted for the remnant of the night Jane wrapped her arms around him and gave him a slight but perceptible hug, as she brushed her cheek on his fulsome beard. As she lay upon her pillows, she was not sure she should have done that.

At first she was too exhausted to drift to sleep, so Jane went back over the revelations of the last hours. Already she found she could not recall much of what Lucian had said. He had said so much. Some of it was reflective, some of it self justifying, some it wistful. But some of his words were astonishing, even devastating. For the most part it was these she remembered. They gave a picture, clear and bright, of how everything fitted together and of the true relationships between those few people who had impacted her life. There were surprises aplenty. Key passages of dialogue were seared into her memory.

Lucian had begun with his life at Cambridge and his left-wing leanings, his abhorrence of fascism, his rejection of totalitarian communism and his enthusiasm for socialism of the kind propagated by the Fabians. These fashionable sympathies were no bar to either academic or civil service advancement. He spoke of his devotion to Mitzi and his acceptance that the sexual difficulties could not be resolved. He claimed it was Mitzi who had suggested a mistress and Jane had no reason to doubt this. He met Diana, who worked in the Foreign Office. He learned that she lived with a semi-invalid, Robert Block, who was her mentor, although they were not married. This domestic irregularity was unknown to their Bromley neighbours, in an era when living together out of wedlock was much tut-tutted and the term *partner*, in the context of people living together, unheard of. Diana was not averse to the notion of a sexual relationship without emotional commitment and neither was Robert, from whom no attempt was made at concealment.

"He was one of the few genuinely tolerant, enlightened and good people I have ever met."

Jane was pleased with that, but it was the answer to her next question, "Where did I come in?" that came as a bombshell.

"Mitzi badly wanted a child. We could have adopted but she wanted not any child but *my* child. I mentioned this to Diana, who came up with the extraordinary, well it seemed so to me extraordinary, proposition. It was that I should make Diana pregnant, but that at birth the baby should be formally adopted by Mitzi and me. In other words surrogacy as it is now known, although I cannot recall any of us using the term."

Jane felt sick. She swallowed. Her voice was small. "What happened?"

"Well it was very distressing. Especially for Mitzi. About three months before you were due, Diana suddenly announced that she wanted to keep the baby. Nothing would change her mind. I felt afterwards that she resented Mitzi, who had become rather managing and possessive, talking of the baby as if it were her own. We all handled the whole thing in the most amateur way. Anyway, there was a falling out, Diana married Robert to give you a proper start and that was that."

The next shock was financial. There was no life assurance when Robert died and his sickness pension died with him. He left only the house in Bromley. Diana, who relied for income on her work and had no family to look after Jane, contacted Lucian. He discussed the crisis with Mitzi, who agreed Lucian should provide sufficient capital to invest to give Diana enough income to bring up the child without having to work. He also paid the school fees. A condition had been that Lucian had access to Jane but since Diana correctly thought this was Mitzi's idea, she refused. Lucian went ahead anyway with the money. So it was his capital from which Jane now enjoyed her income.

"But why did you not contact me after mother died?"

"Because," said Lucian simply, "by then I was myself also dead. I had to wait for the Will process to take effect."

Jane thought of saying "I see", but she thought that might imply approval, so instead she ventured, "What about this fake death of yours? What on earth were you doing?"

Lucian became animated. He had received word through a friend in the French secret service who had been in England on De Gaulle's staff during the war, that plans were being laid to murder him by remnants of The Hastings Option. They feared his intention to write a book exposing their treachery. Lucian faced a life surrounded by bodyguards or a fresh start. He chose the latter. Mitzi agreed. The Frenchman was the fishing companion who organised the drowning. Mitzi knowingly identified remains dumped from a fishing boat. Only the Frenchman, Mitzi and Harold Trubshaw were in the plot. It was Harold's job to establish Lucian as a serial detective writer, and to make him financially secure without allowing a high public profile. He did this very efficiently, but "messed everything up by blabbing about the manuscript. Then he died with extraordinarily bad timing."

This was interesting. "What you mean *blabbing*?"

Lucian was filling his pipe for the third time. After the Zippo ritual he continued.

"Harold wanted to clear the way for quick publication and secure his fees before you inherited. About a year ago, he mentioned it to Bremmer. Unfortunately, some years back Bremmer sold control of the firm to the Flemington family trust company. Unaware of the significance, Bremmer mentioned the manuscript to Oswald Flemington the MP, son of Joseph Flemington of The Hastings Option. Oswald told his son Monty, a nasty piece of work married to your school friend. Monty decided to act and cobbled together a half-official, half-secret and fully ridiculous "ripping yarn" group of people to try and suppress it. They were all men of armchair action, so they appealed to a contact in army intelligence. He organised the secondment of Tim Weldon to do the fieldwork."

"Don't mention that man to me!" exclaimed Jane in a voice shrill with the dismissal of a lover betrayed. Then softer, but with an edge of curiosity, "Why him anyway?"

"I think by chance mostly, but he was shortly to leave the army and go into business, which made him a shrewd choice. Also, he was very good at his job."

Jane's chin dropped to her chest. She studied her hands spread on the table before her. She wanted to say something, but the words would not come. She fought back tears. Lucian, seeing the corners of her mouth twitch, saw his opportunity.

"Jane, you have every reason to despise Tim, but things are not as they seem."

Before Lucian could go further Jane exploded.

"Nothing, absolutely nothing, is as it seems! Even I, me, my family, my whole reason for living, my very existence are not as they seem! You are not! My mother was not! The man whom I thought was my father, was not! Mitzi was not! As for bloody Tim!"

Jane paused. She was exhausted. She should stop Lucian now. No more excuses, explanations, justifications, recasting of characters. What did it matter, this past of hers? It was a shambles of confusion, greed, selfishness and self-interest. If she was to have any hope, any hope at all, of rebuilding her life, it would have to be the kind of life that hung down from its future, not one which grew up from its past. There were those whose whole identity, job, status and perspective were secured to the history of their families. There were others so deprived they had no past at all. Yet it was from this latter group that the great achievers often came. They travelled far because they travelled light. They had no baggage. Jane had baggage to weigh her to a stop. She must dump it. Now! And yet? Jane looked at Lucian, wreathed in his aromatic smoke, his grey eyes narrowed in perception of her turmoil, yet not without a glow of sympathy.

"Go on", she whispered.

Lucian had some surprising things to say. "When Tim broke into Harold's he found a copy of the letter to you. He also found details of the location of this croft and Jock McAllister's address. There was correspondence between Paul Harvey and Harold. It was all in the same drawer as the secret Will. Tim was suspicious. He took everything but showed only the copy of your letter to the gang. Guessing that Lucian, Jock and Paul Harvey were one and the same, he made a secret trip up here to see me. We had not met previously, but I knew his father. He featured in a book I wrote when Lucian Feyrbaeme. Anyhow, when I realised things were getting out of control, I decided to tell Tim everything."

Jane found this hard to take. "Are you saying Tim knew where this place was all along?"

"Yes. The problem was that he could not tell you directly without giving away his connection. He and I decided it would be best to allow Monty and his crew to acquire the manuscript in convincing circumstances, so that they would lose interest in you. Unfortunately they thought it necessary to try and frighten you, so that you would make no complaint when the manuscript disappeared. We were not worried about your wondering what had happened to it, as we planned to tell you the whole story when we had put them off your trail. Their cruel charade at one of the MI6 training centres ruined everything."

Lucian had paused. Jane could tell he knew what she would say next.

"All this does not excuse Tim's behaviour towards me, nor the fact that his burglary killed that old man."

Jane was not sure how to describe the intimacies she had enjoyed, nor whether Lucian knew of them. She hesitated. Lucian laid his pipe on the table, leant forward and took hold of Jane's hand. His grip was gentle.

"Tim is in love with you. One day you will have to accept that. As for Harold, well, the timing was certainly unfortunate, but he was likely to go at any time."

Jane was silent. Accept that? And everything else as well? The rewriting of her whole life? It was all very well for people like Tim and Lucian who both inhabited a world where lies and truth were mixed into a brew of deception, enabling their make-believe to appear reality, but Jane's world was not like that. In comparison to theirs, hers was innocent. It may be naive, isolated, introvert, stupid even. But her world was real.

She looked at Lucian. She saw concern, comfort. She saw, after all, her father. He would have to be her lifeline. Whatever his faults, he, too, was real. He was her only link between the false and the true.

"What about Mitzi?" she said suddenly.

For the first time Lucian appeared to be on the point of losing his composure. He swallowed. His eyes, detected Jane, grew moist. He put his pipe to his mouth, took it away again, then pressed his forefinger to his top lip. Eventually he managed to speak.

"We remained close. We corresponded regularly as Jock the widower, who had met Mitzi the widow on holiday in Venice. We went there every year. We would stay at separate hotels and meet up at Florians for coffee, then spend the days together. The original plan was for Mitzi to take you to Venice, after you had settled in up here and for us both to tell you the truth about yourself. Remember, all the mysteries about the cottage and the manuscript would not have happened because Harold would have told you everything."

Jane was comforted by this. At least it explained why Mitzi was expecting her when she called that day and why Lucian's wife had taken Jane under her wing. It was comforting, too, to detect a seam of emotion running beneath Lucian's thick skin. There were further questions which needed answers, but Jane could take no more now.

"I can't concentrate any more. I need some rest. We can carry on tomorrow." Jane glanced at the clock. "Well, later today."

Lucian nodded. "May I rest here on the sofa? It is hardly worth going home."

Jane acquiesced gracefully then advanced towards her newly found father for the impulsive hug, before climbing the narrow stairs to an uncertain sleep.

At about ten in the morning Jane awoke to the smell of frying bacon. The sun was shining through the small bedroom windows. She listened to the clatter of crockery in the kitchen below. Putting on her flannel dressing-gown she hurried barefoot down the stairs. Lucian greeted her with a wave of a spatula as he stood over the stove.

"Ah, you look rested. Would you like tea or coffee? There is porridge, bacon, sausage and egg. Oatcakes and marmalade to follow."

Jane was astonished. A shopping trip had been on her agenda as supplies were low.

"Where did you get all this stuff?" then softer, "and yes, coffee would be fine."

Lucian pulled an already brimming dish from the oven and added two cooked eggs from the frying pan. "I made an early trip to the Dunvegan store. They open at eight."

Jane sat down at the table bemused. Lucian was now spooning porridge into bowls.

"A good meal will help to soothe your nerves".

Jane ate what was put in front of her. She did not yet feel like talking, though she did manage "I'm sure all this fried food is bad for me, but it tastes wonderful!"

Lucian was sardonic. "Men who live alone for twenty years become good at fry-ups."

In the end Jane came to the point that had been troubling her since she woke up. "What are we going to do about the manuscript? We cannot just let Monty and his friends get away with it."

Lucian's response took Jane by surprise. He had retyped the entire manuscript, with important revision, on to a new word processor the previous year. "So I have it on disc." That was not all.

"You cannot publish until you have re-established your life. That will take two years or so. Then if you choose to, and it is *your* choice still, I will come back from the supposed dead and authenticate it. Tim will come forward to disclose the whole plot to try and silence you. It will be a huge story."

Jane hardly knew what to say. "But won't you be had up for something?"

"I have committed no crime. No one has suffered from my disappearance. All my debts were paid. Even death duties. No contracts were broken." Lucian chuckled. "I have travelled on a passport provided by my French friend from his secret service facility. I suppose they could try and get me for that, but they would only make fools of themselves. They might even try the Official Secrets Act, but that would mean acknowledging everything was official. That would bring down the government!"

Jane sighed. " But Tim? Why is he doing this?"

Lucian stood up from the table and began to gather the dishes.

"First, because he is so appalled by what happened that he actually resigned from the army early." Lucian paused again. He put a handful of crockery into the sink. He then turned to Jane. When he spoke he did so softly but with the emphasis on every word.

"Also because he loves you. He wants to be at your side during what will be something of an ordeal. He knows he let you down before, but he was a serving officer under orders. This time he will be free. He won't fail you a second time."

Jane was astonished. She tried to remain sceptical but it was difficult. This could change everything. There was still one more question.

"One of those awful men said my mother was a communist. Was she?"

Lucian shook his head. "No, she was not a communist. Like me she was a left-winger and I think had some difficulties with her bosses because for a time she worked with the Foreign Office defectors of the 1950's. But she herself was never a communist. Certainly she would never have been a traitor to her country. That was a crafty attempt to confuse you. To make you feel they knew you had secrets which had to be concealed." Lucian shook his head again. "Blackmail. The bastards." His tone was contemptuous.

For a long time Jane sat in silence, her mind absorbing the impact of these last minutes. So she was no longer alone. This time round her life would be quite different. At length she looked up at Lucian, standing with a dishcloth in his hand and awaiting her reaction with a touch of ill conceived anxiety. Jane smiled. She felt her face light up. Now there was hope. She looked straight at Lucian.

"You said you had a passport?"

"Yes. Why?"

"Let's make that trip to Venice."

CHAPTER TWENTY

Three years had passed since the holiday in Venice with Lucian. By day, Jane and Lucian had wandered the sights of this peerless city, fascinated as much by the cool, narrow alleys leading nowhere in particular and crisscrossed by the minor canals, as by the spectacular exhibitions in the art galleries or the Byzantine splendour of St Mark's Cathedral. But it was in the Doge's Palace that Lucian was in his element. With the compulsive enthusiasm of the hobbyist he described not only the palace in detail, but the process of government which had taken place within its walls. The curious but logical processes which had enabled the Venetians to build their enormously wealthy and powerful trading empire. The wily intrigues of government, the thirst for information, the facility to point an accusing finger, the unfamiliar scales of their justice, all of this was a source of fascination to the old man, himself a plotter and intriguer whose instinct for survival must have been shared by those who could rise to the top of this unique republic and stay there.

On sunny afternoons they sat for hours at one of the cafés in St Mark's Square watching the tourists. Jane watched Lucian too, looking distinguished with his grey beard, Panama hat and linen suit, his image sharpened by the leanness of his figure and the twinkle of his eye. As the hammers of the Moors rang out the passing hours, the filial bonds between father and daughter were at last joined, to the soft beat of the café musicians and the glare of the high Venetian sun.

The pair indulged a last extravagance, hiring a water taxi to the airport for their return flight. Jane watched Lucian sitting in the stern of the launch, his Panama clutched in his lap and his white hair flowing in the wind. As the skyline of towers and spires faded, he turned and murmured half to himself, "If I had been born in another place at another time, I should like to have been a Venetian."

Jane thought of all the strange twists and turns of his life and smiled. You would have been in your element, she mused to herself. Shortly Lucian turned to her, his eyes thoughtful.

"Your life, Jane, is painting, not illustrating. Painting."

She nodded. The feast of art of the last two weeks had inspired her creativity.

Lucian leant forward. "But however you spend your life, you must not spend it alone!"

It was autumn now in London. Whilst the holiday months had been a disappointment, the weather this October had turned out to be exceptionally fine and warm. There was a softness in the mid-afternoon air that provided the tourists who had bought the cheap, out of season packages, with a bonus not enjoyed by their richer fellows who had come in the peak.

Jane found herself walking along Piccadilly. She was on her way from the Bond Street Gallery where she now had a permanent exhibition of her paintings, to buy some tickets for a show she wanted to see at the Haymarket Theatre. She preferred to go to the box office to choose the seats from the plan. If the weather had been poor, she would have taken a taxi. She could afford it now, but the sun was inviting and she was in no hurry.

Her painting had taken off, helped by her beautifully illustrated book *Heather and Wild Flowers of the Highlands*, which had become a bestseller the previous Christmas. Earlier this year, one of the smart galleries in Bond Street, specialising in work of contemporary artists, had offered her a small section for a permanent exhibition. From here she was able to sell as many watercolours as she could produce. Once again, her Highland scenes were the most popular. She emulated the great Victorian watercolour artists. This fitted well with the modern trend which made Victorian reproduction smart. The crowning moment had come when two of her paintings had been accepted for the Summer Exhibition at the Royal Academy. The traumatic events of the summer three years ago had retreated into the recesses of her memory, rarely recalled, although when they were, the images and impressions were vivid.

Suddenly Jane saw Celia walking towards her on the pavement. There was no mistaking her anywhere. Jane had tried to get in touch with her when she returned from Skye, but the telephone to the house near Newbury had been disconnected and a later Christmas card was returned marked "Gone Away", so Jane had no idea what had happened to her friend or, indeed, that monster of a husband. Now they were nearly upon each other.

Celia suddenly cried, "Jane, darling! How wonderful!" and almost flew into her arms.

There followed kissing and embraces. As usual, Celia did the talking.

"Darling, you must hear all my news! I know, let's go for tea at Fortnum's! We should be able to get in before the queue builds up."

Jane was not sure. "Have you time?"

"Oh darling, loads. I'm on my way to meet Monty, but it will do him no harm to wait. It'll keep him on his toes."

"How is Monty?" ventured Jane as she trotted obediently beside Celia along the pavement.

"Oh, we had a falling out. Nearly got divorced. Then he came into his money and decided to go into politics, so I made up. I fancy living in Downing Street!"

Jane was aghast. "Downing Street?"

The conversation was interrupted as they arrived at the restaurant. It was not long before they were seated at a window table.

"I'm famished," said Celia, "I missed lunch altogether, I was so busy shopping. So after the sandwiches, I shall have an eclair." Then, "Yes darling. He has found a safe seat already. He will be in at the next election, and with his money and patronage he will become leader of the party before long. You wait and see!"

"Oh," said Jane. This was appalling news. She decided to probe for more, doing her best to sound conversational rather than interested.

"What made Monty go into politics? I mean with all that money, you would think you would both want to be free. You know, the press and everything. Always trying to catch you out."

"Oh no dear. Monty wants to establish a political dynasty. He will be the third generation. It means I will have to have babies, which I hate, but I will hire an army of nannies, so that I barely ever see them, and then only at their best."

"Ah," said Jane, "I see." More, she thought to her herself, than meets the eye.

For the next twenty minutes, between mouthfuls of cucumber sandwich and eclair, Celia prattled on about her new life in politics. Jane wondered how such a vacuous brain would manage. Knowing Celia, the trick would be to learn a few catchphrases and buzzwords to scatter through her conversation, to give the impression, quite false, that she knew what she was talking about. If I did that, thought Jane, I would appear an imbecile, but somehow Celia will carry it off with dazzling success. At last Celia finished eating and her propaganda show appeared to be over. She looked at Jane with sudden interest.

"Darling, before I ran off and left temporarily, Monty told me some peculiar story that you had suddenly inherited some sort of mystery. He said it could be quite valuable. I didn't really pay attention as we were at the ignoring each other stage, but what was it exactly?"

Jane looked at Celia. "In a manner of speaking, it was a key."

"A key? What sort of key?"

A Gift of Treason

Jane thought for a moment.

"The key to life."

"Oh darling! What fun!"

Celia's exclamation betrayed she was out of her depth. She changed tack.

"What about that author you met in the pub?"

"Yes?"

"Did you ever see him again?"

"Yes."

"What happened to him in the end?"

Jane drifted back to that November day after Venice, when she had made a last visit to Skye before the winter. It was a Sunday and Lucian had suggested she join him for lunch at his house outside Portree. When Jane arrived, she noticed a new Japanese four-wheel drive parked outside. Lucian did all his own cooking and housekeeping, but there was no sign of him in the house. Jane found a note on the kitchen table. *We are walking on the beach.* We?

She went through the little gate at the bottom of the garden and followed the winding path to the shore. There, in the distance, she saw the two of them. Lucian she could recognise immediately, but she was not certain about the other. They separated when they spotted her, and the second man walked towards her. Even before she could see for sure, she knew it was Tim. Jane was caught off guard. She had known she would have to make a decision soon. But she had been putting it off. Now the moment of truth could be delayed no longer. It was only seconds away. Jane felt her heart racing.

Jane surfaced from her reverie as Celia repeated her question.

"Well dear, what happened to him?"

"Happened?"

"Yes!"

Jane looked at her watch. There would just be time.

"Celia, wait here a moment. I must make a quick telephone call."

"But darling!" Celia waved a despairing hand.

Jane hurried to the payphone. She rang *The Sentinel* and caught Nick, who was now Features Editor, just before the afternoon conference. They had maintained contact and Jane had promised Nick the story when she was ready. Publication of *The Hastings Option* would follow on the back of the story of Monty and his crude efforts to silence history.

"Nick, I am ready"

"Are you sure?"

"Yes."

"And Lucian and Tim?"

"More than!"

"Okay, I'll call you at home tonight. Will you be in?"

"Yes."

"And Jane…"

"Yes?"

"You know this will be big. Very big."

"Yes."

When she returned to the table Jane was lost in thought. Celia was looking impatient.

"Jane dear, I've just remembered. We're dining at the Carlton Club. I must fly. You can tell me about the author next time. Do let's keep in touch!"

Another kiss and she was gone.

The author?

Then Jane remembered.

She smiled.

"He's my husband," she murmured softly to herself.